Hector

&

Amalia

Hector

&

Amalia

Dea A. Myers

1st Edition

Thanks...

To God, the Father, the Son and the Holy Spirit. All glory to You! You are the One who carries me through cloudy waters. To Chris Myers for all his dedication to this project, especially with his sport writing expertise. To all of those who support and pray for our ministry, a BIG thanks! To my kiddos, family and friends, I am grateful for each one of you. Dea A. Myers

Prologue

The two Worlds of Cotton County

The story of Hector and Amalia cannot be fully understood without the history of the town where they grew up. Located in the southern part of the US, and part of Cotton County, Trendville is a charming town of twenty-five thousand people.

Trendville was officially founded in 1921 by a group of farmers, who wanted more than land, they wanted a tight community in which they could count on in times of trouble. Prior to its foundation, it was nothing but a long set of farms. So the farmers donated a part of their land to the town and created a town council to manage together the city's priorities and its needs.

The town was founded, and other farmers tried to join them. Since their lands were mostly cotton plantations, they decided to create a county called Cotton County. Together, they survived the great depression and the Second World War. With their unity and hard work, they were able to not only survive, but also thrive.

Little by little, the former farm conglomerate saw the first elementary school, doctor's office and bank coming together. The downtown land was donated by four farmers, whose lands were right in the middle of the map of the town. Each of them donated a corner of their lands, and right in the middle of the map, downtown started to be created.

The streets were named after the farmers, who donated the land, and the story of the town was passed on from generation to generation. Fast food restaurants and chain stores were left outside of the towns' limits. The town shops were locally owned, and the farmers also sold their products at the farmer's market.

Life in Trendville was good, but it changed with time. Some of the founding farmers passed away and left their land for their children. Sadly, despite knowing their parents' desires, some of them decided to sell their families' properties. Suddenly, the once collaborative town hall meetings became a feud between heritage and progress.

Ben de Souza was the leader of the farmers in the town, and Andrew Larkin was the one pushing for modernizing the city. Everyone knew the council meetings would be intense if the two of them were present.

Mr. de Souza and Mr. Larkin used to be friends when they played for the same high school football team. In fact, they were regional champions their senior year, an accomplishment the town never forgot.

Their grievances started in 2005 when Mr. Larkin used all his prestige and influence to convince the town council to authorize a project, which, according to him, would benefit the whole town. He would build apartment complexes for the needy people, which in the future would benefit the town, since Trendville was growing and could possibly have housing problems.

Mr. Souza's father at the time was the leader of the farmers and asked Mr. Larkin to show them the project's plans, but he convinced the council the construction plans were not necessary, since the whole town knew and trusted him.

The project was approved, and the construction happened, but in a very different way Mr. Larkin told the council. Instead of building houses for the regular citizens, he built upscale mansions and luxury homes to sell to the rich people in the nearby city. These were people who were tired of the traffic, violence and all the chaos a big city had to offer.

Needless to say Mr. Larkin made millions through the sales of these properties and the whole town changed in no time. Mr. Larkin bought more and more land and constructed many more mansions. In a blink of an eye, Trendville was divided into two worlds - Half was rural, and the other part was luxurious, rich and fancy. The new citizens started to participate in meetings, demanding changes be made in town.

They all felt betrayed, especially Mr. De Souza, who considered Andrew Larkin a friend. The argumentative, but civil council meetings became part of the past. In 2009 the new citizens demanded authorization from the council to build their own private and elitist school for their children, since they didn't want their kids to attend the public school. Mr. De Souza argued if they granted such authorization the abyss between the two halves of the town would be even bigger and the children would have to deal with it from an early age. By a vote of 3 to 2, the city council voted against the construction of the new school.

The town council's intentions were good, but it didn't accomplish much since their school naturally ended up divided in two groups: The *haves* and *have nots*. From an early age, the wealthy interacted with others like themselves, and the lower middle-class ones had no choice but to form their own groups.

Mr. Souza could not forgive himself for trusting Andrew in that meeting. He had to see his daughter Amalia coming home so many times feeling less and smaller because of bullying and things they could not afford. Mr. Larkin, otherwise, hadn't given up on getting rid of the farmers and making more money with new luxury homes to be built. He was proud of how his son Hector was confident, popular and strong as he himself was, twenty years before.

Mr. Souza and Mr. Larkin, the *haves* and *have nots* unofficial leaders had no idea, but their worlds were about to collide once again... This time not because of sports or having the same goals, but because Hector and Amalia were about to meet... And about to fall in love.

Week One

Worlds Colliding

Amalia

Week One – Day One - Monday

Just a Bad Day

It was early morning when Amalia woke up to go to school. It was the week prior to the holiday week. Amalia was always an enthusiast of Thanksgiving, but that year would be the first year her grandma wouldn't be around. As much as she wanted to be positive and hope for the best, Amalia knew it would take a toll on her mother, who was already struggling on a regular basis, nevertheless on a holiday her mother and grandmother used to cook and work together.

Amalia looked through the window and saw the sun shining timidly on the back of her house. Despite having grown up in a farmhouse her entire life, she never became tired of that view. She was lost in her thoughts when her father knocked on the door.

"Pumpkin, it is time for school. Mom prepared breakfast. You better show up". he said, reminding her and left.

Behind the doors, Amalia knew she had to hurry up since those were probably one of the days her mother was in a manic state of depression and decided to cook all the house pantry. She knew well what would come after the manic state, the melancholy and discouragement would invade her mother's heart. Amalia took a deep breath... She didn't want to make matters worse for her mother, so she needed to hurry up in order to get to the table.

Amalia got dressed, grabbed her phone, backpack and earplugs and was almost leaving the room when she looked at the board on the wall and realized she had a test that morning. She really had to hurry up.

Amalia sat at the table to eat with her mother, father, and Rafael, her eleven-year-old brother, who loved to push all her buttons at once. She looked at the table and felt discouraged. There was so much food on the table she would never be able to eat all of it. There was fruit from their garden, three types of Portuguese bread, homemade jam, biscuits, and cinnamon rolls.

"Eat it all. Breakfast is the most important meal of the day," her mother said. Amalia asked herself if this was really true, since many of her friends didn't have breakfast and they seemed fine to her.

"Let's make a deal. One cup of latte and a biscuit and I will take the rest to school with me," Amalia said, trying to solve the situation without causing an argument, she definitely didn't want to let her mother down. "I also have a test so I can't be late."

"Ok. A cup of latte and a biscuit and you take the rest to school."

"Awesome," Amalia said excitedly so she could finally leave the house.

"Ah, big sister, I almost forgot to tell you... I put your name down to dance traditional Portuguese dance at my school on Friday for the cultural fair. The teacher will give me extra two points for that, isn't it great?" Rafael told the news as if they were great and Amalia was in shock. He had to be joking.

"Oh Rafa, it is so beautiful you thought of your sister to represent our Portuguese heritage at the fair. I am so touched by it," their mother said excitedly, while Amalia started to feel sick to her stomach.

That couldn't be happening. She already had to deal with the fact she was the weirdo of the school, dancing in front of everyone in a traditional Portuguese outfit at her brother's school would definitely take her to YouTube and social media in no time and in a very negative way. That invitation had to be a joke.

"Well, you should have asked before because I think I will have an appointment on Friday," she said, thinking any appointment would be better than dancing at Rafael's school.

"What kind of appointment is that? You are always home on Fridays," her brother asked with a smirky smile on his face.

"I really gotta go! Will talk later about that," she said, putting the food container in her bag and heading to the door.

Her father asked if she needed a ride, but she declined, all she wanted was to disappear before being backed into a corner.

Amalia hopped on her bike. She was going to put in her earplugs when she listened to her mom yelling from the house. "Don't wear earplugs!" And off she went to school.

Her mind was racing fast while she rode the bike to school. Of course Rafael would bring this up in the middle of the breakfast and in front of their mother, who was Portuguese, so she would not be able to say no. She was boiling inside. God had to have a sense of humor when he put a brother like Rafael in her life.

She ended up in a rough spot. If she really said no, her mom would be disappointed with her, and if she said yes, there would be like a thousand percent certainty she would be the laughingstock for the year in her school.

She parked her bicycle in front of the high school building and took a deep breath. There she was in front of the building, a mixture of earthly hell and paradise called *High School.* For all her school life, Amalia dreamed about getting into high school, for the friends, the cute boys, the prom, the drama clubs, and the extracurricular activities, but her life itself in that school was a drama.

Amalia's high school was divided into two social tribes, the *haves* and the *have nots.* Needless to say the two groups hated one another. Her high school was a sample of the town she lived in.

Her town was close to a big city and was once a place with exclusively small farmers, like her father, but in recent years her city was invaded by people who worked in the city but wanted to live in a calm and safe neighborhood.

The huge mansions and large houses started to pop up year after year and the town was divided. Technically, they all belonged to the same zip code, but the truth was they belonged to two different realities.

For Amalia, the *have* girls were mean, and the cute boys would never look at her, since she clearly wasn't one of them. Luckily for Amalia, her *have nots* friends were amazing. They made up for all the bad things she had to endure daily. She entered the class and sat in her usual seat, close to her friends.

"I totally forgot about the test today," she confessed, worried.

"Let me write down the basics for you so you won't do so bad," Little told her.

Little was her best friend since third grade. She once was a preemie baby and her mother named her "Little", but she started to grow crazily since then and became one of the tallest girls on the basketball team. Yet, she had to live with the fact she would be called "Little" for the rest of her life.

"Thank you!" Amalia said heart warmed by her empathy. Little was not only a strong, tall black girl, but was an A-plus student. She really had a brain and was always competing in math, physics, and chemistry competitions. So, having some notes from her would make Amalia more confident.

Lunchtime arrived finally and they all sat down at their usual table to eat. They were all there. Little, Amalia, Alfred, whose body type was not athletic at all and dreamed of being a filmmaker, and there was Alex, who was always dressed like a rapper to seem cool, but in fact was a nerd, who loved video games and was an expert playing them.

"I got some food my mom cooked for breakfast. It is too much. Do you want some?". Amalia offered.

"Oh my goodness, I love your mom's food! I want some for sure! Whatever it is, I am going to like it!" Little said excited.

"Yo man, it sounds cool," Alex said, trying to use his rapper's fabricated voice, but it didn't last long since the game nerd inside of him showed up.

"Do you know your mom's food looks like the princess food in the medieval game I play?" Alex asked and started talking non-stop about this game he was playing. They all looked at one another and started to laugh. "What?" Alex asked, offended.

"You are such a nerd, Al," Little observed.

"I am not a nerd. I am gangsta," he said, and they all started to laugh.

"Sure. We all saw you running away from the lizards at the zoo," Amalia recalled.

"C'mon, give me a break! That was in 4th grade and for the record, that lizard looked like a dinosaur."

"Ok, brave guy. I have to go; I need to take a look at Little's notes before the test begins."

Amalia made it to her seat in the classroom. She started reading Little's notes and was starting to freak out. She hated chemistry, hated. She didn't see any purpose for any regular person to study the subject. In her opinion the only people who needed it were scientists and people who would work with it. Not her.

She tried to memorize the molecules of the chemical elements. Everything looked alike, one dash in the wrong place and it was over. She looked at them several times and hoped to remember them before the test.

Little arrived in class and sat in front of Amalia as she always did. The teacher, Mrs. Hawthorn, walked into class, and she was not in a good mood that day. She asked for silence and reminded the class she would never accept any type of cheating in her classroom.

Amalia knew she wasn't talking to her, because her grades were not amazing, but they were hers, besides she would never do such a thing. She was fixing her pen and eraser on the top of her desk when she heard her name:

"I hope I was clear about it, Amalia," she said, and Amalia immediately felt sick to her stomach. "You know what? I really don't want to get upset today. Little, change places with Clay, please. Now!" Mrs. Hawthorn said as if she was trying to prevent Amalia and Little cheating on the test.

Little and Amalia looked at each other as if they were trying to understand what was going on, and Little left, sitting on Clay's usual seat.

The test started and Amalia still had that knot in her stomach. She was already not good at chemistry. She studied at the last minute for the test and now the teacher was suspicious about her. She hoped at least the test was multiple choice, so she could remember what she studied. She turned the front page of the booklet, and realized they were open questions, meaning she would have to draw them out of nowhere.

Before she could realize all those letters, numbers, bars and what she called "honeycombs" were all mixed up in her mind and she couldn't remember a single one of them. As she was listening to the big clock in front of the classroom ticking, she hoped for a miracle. She couldn't stop thinking of her parents and the high expectations they had for her. They would be absolutely disappointed with the test result, and she definitely hated disappointing them.

Twenty minutes later, Amalia was the first to finish the test. She answered all the questions but wasn't confident about any of them. She just wanted to disappear and run away to her home, but getting home after such a bad test wouldn't be any easier.

Amalia was so down she didn't want to see or talk to anyone. She decided to hide in the bathroom for a couple minutes. The restroom was empty, and she went to the last stall. She sat on the top of the toilet and latched the door. It would be the best place for her to calm down and hide before going back home.

Amalia

Week One – Day One - Monday

Restroom Confessions

While in the restroom, Amalia heard the door open, and then, two female voices. It was impossible to not recognize the voices of those two *have* girls from her classroom.

"Did you get the answers? I pretended to pick up an eraser on the floor so you could see it," Abby asked excitedly.

"Yes. I did what you said. Copied everything and burned one of the answers so we wouldn't have equal tests," Kat said even more excited.

"You have no idea what I have done before the test. I went to the teacher's room and told Mrs. Hawthorn I wasn't sure, but I thought I had heard Amalia and Little talking about cheating on the test," Abby said, and Kat started laughing.

"That was genius! While Mrs. Hawthorn was distracted with the two *have nots*, we were free to share our answers."

They went on talking and Amalia couldn't believe what she was hearing. How could they possibly do something like that? She was absolutely shocked by their evil acts. She pulled out her phone carefully from her backpack, maybe there would be still time to catch them saying some of it. She then muted the phone completely and started to record. She thought it wouldn't hurt to try.

Amalia held the phone for a couple seconds and they started to talk about makeup, and she knew she had missed the opportunity to record them. She was almost turning off the phone when a third *have* girl, Mel, arrived. And as a strike of luck, they all started to talk excitedly about the test all over again and Amalia didn't miss a thing this time.

She finished recording them and started to be concerned about herself. How was she going to leave the bathroom with them there? What if they found out she was there this whole time? She would definitely be in trouble. She was thinking about it when a new group of girls arrived at the bathroom, a group of six, meaning more people were leaving the test. The *have* girls left, and Amalia was finally able to leave the bathroom.

She left the bathroom and definitely didn't want to talk to anyone. She had never hidden anything from Little before, but she knew she had to do it. After being bullied for so many years by the *have* girls, she knew Little wouldn't blink once before surrendering that recording to the teacher.

Yes, Amalia felt extremely tempted to do the same, but in her heart, she didn't know if it was the right thing to do or not. She texted Little saying she needed to hurry home, and they would talk later. She hopped on her bike and went home as fast as she could. After bombing a test and recording the *haves* confession, all she needed was the comfort of her home.

She got home and her mother told her to wash up because she was setting the table so they could all eat together. She made a Portuguese soup called Caldo Verde, (green stew maybe in English?), she wasn't sure. She loved the soup, but her brother Rafael would do anything to get away from it.

"I don't want it. It is green. Who wants to eat green food?" he complained.

"It is good for you, little brother. Very healthy," she said and smiled, putting him in a tough spot.

"What about the traditional Portuguese dance in the school, big sister? I already told the teacher you would do it. Mom even found her traditional outfit for the dance," he said with a sly smile.

Kudos to him because she had totally forgotten about the dance at his school. To make matters worse, her mom was looking at her with sparkling eyes.

"Are you going to do it?" her mother asked in a sweet way, and she couldn't say no. Maybe that would help her when she found out she bombed the test.

"Sure, I will do it,"

After dinner, Amalia went to the back of the house, to the place her father had built for her to practice her dancing.

The view was absolutely stunning that evening. The pavement she used to dance on, the cotton plantation and the sunset in the back inspired her even more. Amalia got her phone and her speaker. She was practicing for a national competition of worship dance. She loved to dance, but that night she wanted to do it more than ever.

She loved dancing for God. Her body, her movements, all of it spoke to God what her words couldn't sometimes.

The song was playing, and at that time it was exactly what Amalia needed. To be reminded even in the worst moments, God still loved her. She didn't know what to do with the recording, or if someone would bully her because of the dance at Rafael's school, or how her grades would be after that terrible result, but that night she only wanted to dance to God.

Hector

Week One – Day One - Monday

Early Morning

It was five in the morning and Hector was sleeping heavily when his father woke him up, scaring him. He looked at the clock and could not believe his father woke him at five and was already so energetic.

"Dad! It is five in the morning!" Hector protested.

"I know, but if I am up, you can do it too! You are this close to winning the championship. You have to give it your best now. It is now or never!" His father said enthusiastically.

Hector finally sat up and started to put on his sweatpants and sneakers since he knew he wouldn't be left alone until conceded to his father's appeals.

They went to the basement. Hector got a bottle of sparkling water and had a sip before he started training. His father went to the elliptical while he was on the treadmill. They finished the treadmill, and they started to work on the weights they had at home. After that, his father turned on the 50-inch TV they had in the *Basement Gym*, as they called it, and started to follow a subscription for exercise series, which would work their body as a whole.

They finished the training session, and they were both exhausted. It was impressive at the age of 48 his father was still able to keep up with all those programs. Hector sat on the sofa, and he was cleaning his face with a towel when his father got closer to him and told him his numbers.

"So, you did great on the treadmill, but your numbers were not as good as yesterday on peloton,"

"C'mon dad, I was not even up. We've been here for two hours, and I have a test today!"

"Stop whining, H.! I wish I had the life you have today. I built a whole, fully equipped gym for you here in the basement and you are complaining?! I used to practice when it was still dark, sometimes in the rain, without any sort of comfort and I won the title," he said and made a brief pause.

"You know what? That's what we should do today, you can run to school instead of driving the truck," Drew suggested.

"I can't, dad! I have a test today, and I have practice after school,"

"What kind of test do you have today?" his father asked. Hector Told him he would have a chemistry test.

"Chemistry?! Give me a break, H.! You can do this test with your eyes closed," he took a pause and said, "Okay. We will practice outdoors another time."

Hector went upstairs to his own bathroom. He was still sleepy and felt exhausted. The day had just started, and he would still have chemistry test, and football practice after school, so he definitely needed to be alert.

He got ready and left the house. He hopped in the brand-new truck his father gave him, turned on the engine and also his phone, only to find out there were at least 30 messages from Katherine, or Kat, as she was known, who happened to be his girlfriend for the last three months.

He took a deep breath, "Why in the world would she call him and message him so many times?" His thoughts exactly. He started to read the first text message and felt totally discouraged when he read "We need to talk." Great, he thought, now he would not only have school, tests, practice, the championship, his dad to deal with and now a relationship talk with Kat.

In truth, he also wanted to talk to Kat, but for a different reason. Since the previous week, he had been trying to find the right opportunity to break up with her, but this opportunity never came up.

Kat was beautiful, smart, tall, perfect hair, smile and measurements. Along with her father being friends with his father, they looked good in the pictures, were always on the school social media, and were known as H&K, the upscale couple.

He admitted he liked the attention, but in the previous month, his feelings for Kat were simply fading away and he didn't know how to change it. He didn't want to kiss her or be around her. He couldn't explain it but that's exactly how he felt. He hoped his friends would be there as soon as he arrived so he could avoid the conversation so early in the morning.

He parked the truck in the parking lot, and as he predicted, his friends were there - Clay, Jace and JC, came to greet him.

"JC's parents are out of town. We are going to watch a game tomorrow after the practice. Are you up for it?" Jace approached excitedly.

"Umm, it depends. Is it just going to be us or are you guys thinking of inviting someone else?" Hector asked, afraid a simple game could turn into a wild party or Kat could be there.

"No man, just us. Low key. No girls talking during the game. Just us," Jace said, and Hector hoped that was the case.

"Count me in then," he finally said.

Lunchtime arrived and Kat and her friends showed up to eat with them as they always did. Kat, Abby and Mel, who were Hector, Jace and JC's girlfriends, respectively. As always, they spent the majority of the time talking about the championship. Hector and Kat seemed slightly uncomfortable with one another.

When they all finished lunch, Abby left, saying she needed to find Mrs. Hawthorn, while Hector and Kat went to the bin to place their leftovers.

"You called 30 times, Kat. What did you want to talk about?" Hector asked not wanting to, but eeling he had to do it.

"Chemistry. I was desperate, I am good at shopping, makeup, fashion, but I panic with chemistry."

"Sorry. My dad woke me up at five in the morning to practice. I just saw it when I was on the way," he explained.

"It's okay. I called Abby and I am fine now. I feel confident about the test."

"Good,"

"See you tonight?" she asked.

"Wednesday. I have practice today and woke up early," he said, kissed her very briefly and left.

After their talk, Hector went back to his classroom and had a good feeling when he finished the chemistry test.

Hector

Week One - Day One – Monday

Mystery Girl

After school was over, he went to the locker room to change clothes and put on the gear he needed for practice. As always, Jace and JC were telling jokes before practice, imitating one player of the opponent team from their last game, and the funny faces he made during the game. They all started laughing.

"He was trying to put up an intimidating face, but it was, in fact, a funny face. Man, I just wanted to laugh," Jace said. They all laughed because they all knew the player and knew how he was faking a brave face during the game.

"Silly face or not, they almost won the game," Hector noted.

"That's true," JC agreed. "But it is still funny!"

They were all laughing and getting ready to go to the field, when Clay, another player, showed up.

"Hey Hector, isn't that man your father arguing with the coach? I know it is way over there, but it looks like him," Clay observed, looking through the window.

Hector left the locker room and ran to the corner of the field where his father was in a heated conversation with the coach. He felt so embarrassed his father had the guts to do something like that. He loved Coach Johnson, as he was a great coach and was working hard to win a championship> He couldn't believe his father was doing this. He got closer to them and said:

"Do you want us to start to warm up, coach? I guess it is going to rain," Hector asked, trying to put an end to whatever that conversation was.

"I guess it's a great idea," Coach Johnson said and turned to his father. "Mr. Larkin, I really have to go,"

"Can I have a word with my son?" Hector's father asked and the coach nodded, leaving the two alone afterwards.

"Dad, what are you doing here?" Hector asked embarrassed.

"What am I doing here? Trying to save this team from another failure. I am a donor, an alumnus, and a former champion. If they like my money, they should listen to my opinions,"

"Dad, this is not fair! He cannot play for the players, but he is doing all the rest! Coach Johnson is doing a great job!" Hector stressed.

"Listen to me Hector, you are going to win this championship! It doesn't matter who you have to push, or what you have to do, you are going to make it happen," he said and left, leaving Hector devastated.

It was hard for Hector to keep his mind on the practice that afternoon. It was noticeable. Jace and JC continued with the jokes, but Hector wasn't in the mood anymore. Coach Johnson saw he was having a terrible performance and dismissed him before the practice was over.

Hector left the practice, went to the locker room, and changed clothes. He hopped in his truck, parked it in a hidden place around the park, locked the car and took a nap. He didn't want to go back home, because if his father saw him arriving home early, he probably wouldn't be happy.

He woke up and realized it was dark. He decided to change routes to go home. He was driving through the rural area of the town when he saw a girl dancing from afar, in front of the cotton field. Her hair floated in the wind while she danced so beautifully and so freely.

Her clothing seemed to blend with her movements. It started to rain, or sprinkle, as many would say. From a distance, the cotton flowers in the dark seemed like snow suspended in the air.

He stopped the truck and kept watching her, as he was absolutely attracted by the sight of her. He had no idea who she was, but she seemed to be free in a way he had never been.

He was intrigued by the fact he couldn't remember her. Trendville was a place in which everyone knew everyone. They had to have met before. But who was she? He absolutely needed to find it out.

His father messaged him asking where he was, and he knew it was time to go home. He turned on the truck and went back to his house.

Amalia

Week One - Day Two - Tuesday

A Bold Move

Amalia woke up feeling good until she remembered everything that had happened the day before. She grabbed her phone that was on her bedside table and found the video she recorded in the school restroom. What was she going to do with it? That was the question occupying her mind. She didn't know what to do, but one thing she knew, the video could not be easily accessed on her phone. She uploaded her video to the cloud, rewatched it to confirm it was really there and deleted it from her phone.

She was still devastated about the chemistry test, but at least she would have an English test that morning and she absolutely loved literature. She was confident it would go well.

She sat at the table for breakfast and to her surprise, her mother had not fallen into a depressive mode. In fact, she was even more excited than the day before. She brought her own Portuguese traditional outfit, so Amalia would wear it. Amalia remembered the outfit from a photo she saw of her mother wearing it when she was a teen. It was touching for Amalia to see how her mother was excited about it. She put some food in her backpack, climbed her bike and left for school. It was definitely time to go.

The English test was first thing in the morning, and she was confident she has done well. It was refreshing to know the previous bad day at school was behind her, and she was definitely ready for good things to happen from that day on.

Amalia was in good spirits, but as soon she and her friends arrived in the lunchroom, they realized they had a problem. The table they were used to eating at for the last three years was gone. Apparently, it broke and the only table available was close to the *haves* people. They looked at each other and decided to face it together since there were no other free tables to sit in their usual area.

They sat and could feel the looks towards them, as if they were saying, "What are you doing here?" There was this uncomfortable atmosphere, but they ended up forgetting about it and enjoying their time together. When Little went to the restroom, Kat, Mel and Abby stopped by to talk to the rest of them.

"What are you *losers* doing here?" Kat asked, provoking them all. "Do you need a map so you can go to your *area*?"

"They said our table was broken," Alfred answered her.

"Well, I hope it doesn't happen anymore. We don't want your loser vibe around". Abby threatened them and they went silent.

Amalia looked at her friends and they seemed so discouraged it hurt her.

"At least we are not cheaters," Amalia said impulsively, while Kat, Abby and Mel froze. They knew *she knew* what had happened the day before. "Now, leave us alone, please,". Amalia asked and they left silently.

Little came back from the bathroom and the others were all excited since Amalia had silenced them with two sentences. It was definitely a victory for the *have nots* people. Amalia just hoped she didn't have to pay a high price for her boldness.

Amalia left school and hopped on her bicycle when Little approached her. She knew she could not avoid that conversation anymore.

"The boys told me you told them they were cheaters. Are they cheating on their popular sporty boyfriends? You knew this and you didn't tell me anything?" Little confronted her.

"It is not that type of cheating. And I have proof, so they left," Amalia finally told her.

"That's why you were avoiding me yesterday," Little concluded.

"Wait a minute. So, they cheated yesterday while we were treated as criminals, and you didn't surrender the proof? Let's do this now! Let's bring some justice to this school! We'll go together," Little said forcefully.

"That's exactly my problem. I don't want to do this out of revenge, if I do this is because I settled in my mind this is the right thing to do," Amalia tried to explain to her.

"You are joking with me! These girls have been treating us like garbage since third grade, humiliating us publicly and when you have the chance to fight them back, you won't do it? This gotta be a joke!" Little said infuriated.

"I see what you are saying, but I need to think about it," Amalia said, torn.

Little continued in her quest to convince Amalia to surrender the proof she had, but Amalia asked her for some space and said she had to go.

Amalia was relieved to finally leave the school. When she was out of the urban area, she stopped the bike, put her earplugs on and started to listen to her favorite songs. She knew her mother advised her not to do so, but it was so close to her house it wouldn't harm her. She started to sing one of her favorite songs when something hit her bike abruptly and she fell to the ground.

Hector

Week One - Day Two - Tuesday

A Bad Day

Hector had no other choice but to run a couple miles with his father early in the morning. He convinced his father to walk around the mysterious girl's property. Maybe he could see her again, he thought. The house definitely looked different in the daylight, but he could surely identify the cotton field in the back and the pavement she danced on the evening before. The house was there but no sign of her.

"Why did you stop?" his father asked, confused.

"To take a break. Cotton fields are beautiful don't you think?" he asked, trying to find the number of her house.

"Winning games is beautiful, H.! We need to keep going. You have a game next Friday,"

Hector kept walking, but when he looked back for the last time, he saw the number of the house on the other side of the mailbox - "Green Street, 318". He started to repeat mentally to himself, so he could find more about her on Google. He went back home, had a shower, and started to get ready for school. He would continue his search later.

As soon as he got to school, he saw Kat waiting for him to arrive. He forgot all about Kat. She left a message saying they needed to talk early in the morning. They walked together to the library since none of their friends used to go to the library, so it would be the perfect spot to talk in private. She asked him what was going on with him.

"I don't know Kat. There is too much in my mind. The games, my dad putting pressure on me to win this championship, no matter what, and I don't think we are working. I think it is time to pull the plug on it," he spoke from his heart.

"What do you mean? We are perfect for each other. Our parents are friends, we grew up together, we have the same friends, we are beautiful together and popular too. We have a whole golden future ahead of us. You are going to take your father's realtor business, and I am going to take my father's appraisal business. How can you say this?" Kat asked, upset.

"That's the point, Kat. Technically, we are perfect for each other, but this is just not working, and please don't you tell this is just me, because I know it is not,"

"We can do couple's therapy. My mom and my dad do this all the time," she suggested it and he was appalled.

"Kat, we are in high school. I'm not doing it,"

"You know what? You are the one who should be begging to be with me. As soon as we break up all the boys of this school will be after me, after being the new *you*," she said in such a confident way it hurt his pride, but the decision was made, and he was not backing down this time.

They were both silent for some time when Kat finally said,

"By all means I am the one who broke up with you, not the opposite," she set her condition.

"Okay," Hector agreed.

Hector went to his class and as soon as he saw the English teacher with a block of papers in her hands, he remembered he had an English test. This immediately worried him. The teacher started saying this test would be different - Grammar, literature and writing would be integrated, with all of it flowing from a Bob Dylan song. Hector immediately started to sweat. He knew it wouldn't end up well for him.

He took a deep breath and started to read the song. He was almost freaking out, since he read it three times and couldn't make out what he meant with that song. Because of this, he couldn't answer the text comprehension questions, and nevertheless write about the song since he had no idea what the song meant. How could people understand that? How? He thought. It didn't make any sense to him.

The only questions he could confidently answer were the ones about grammar, but the rest either was blank, or he guessed. He ended up being the first person to return the test to the teacher and left the room.

Not long after, JC and Jace joined him in his suffering.

"What the heck was that? And who the heck is Bob Dylan?" JC asked, shocked.

"I guess I heard my grandpa talking about him, or something like that, but who cares for Bob Dylan? My dad is going to kill me when he sees my English grade. That's not going to be pretty," Jace confessed.

"That was the worst English test of my life," Hector added, discouraged.

Hector was definitely having a bad day. First, he broke up with Kat, and as much as he was sure of what he was doing, he knew now he didn't have her to comfort him or make him laugh anymore. He was not regretting the decision, but now he was realizing it was tougher than he thought it would be. He was definitely not hungry and didn't want to be around Kat in the lunchroom, so he went to the library, grabbed his phone and read the devotional his pastor sent to the church every day.

The devotional talked about being brave, courageous and about not allowing discouragement to drag you down. It was exactly what he needed. He said a prayer and asked God to show him if he did the right thing or not, of breaking up with Kat.

At the end of the school day, he received a text from the assistant coach saying there was a water leak at the football field, and they would have to cancel practice. He texted JC and Jace, telling them he was going to Jace's house to watch the game later, but he needed to go home first.

He jumped in his truck, turned on the ignition and started driving home when he stopped at the traffic light. He saw a mother crossing the street with her little daughter in her ballet outfit and it made him smile and think about the mystery girl. Did she get one of those when she was a child like that little girl did? He realized he didn't want to go home, but clearly, he would like to at least try to see who that girl was. If he went fast, he could possibly get to the house before her.

He went as fast as he could and before he realized, he was at Green Street- 318, waiting for her. "This mystery has to end today," he thought. He parked the car on the opposite side of her house, between properties so it wouldn't look so suspicious, while he was hoping he would be able to see her soon.

He waited for quite some time and finally saw on the other side of the street an average girl with a bun in her hair riding her bike with a backpack on. Suddenly, he saw Kat's car on the street. How did she find out he was there? Then he saw her stopping the car behind the girl as she was gathering courage to do something. He realized, then, she didn't know he was there.

He saw Kat turn on the engine and hit the girl on the bicycle. Kat left the car while the girl was lying on the street and stepped on her phone. She jumped back in her car and drove off.

Everything was so unpredictable and happened so fast he had no time to think about it. His heart was racing fast, while he was still in shock. Kat had just hit the girl on purpose. If what he had just witnessed was not an answer to his prayers, he didn't know what else could be.

He crossed the street to help the girl. She was lying down on the street. He got closer and remembered her from school, a girl from the *have nots* part of the school. Amalia. She usually had a bun in her hair, but she was different than usual this time. The bun was gone, and he could see her long and wavy hair molding her face. He was surprised but knew then it was her. Amalia was the girl who was beautifully dancing the other night.

Hector & Amalia.

Week One - Day Two - Tuesday

Two Worlds Colliding

He got closer and called to her nervously, "Can you hear me? Are you ok?" If she didn't answer, he would have to call 911.

Amalia opened her eyes and saw Hector looking at her. He seemed concerned. She felt miserable, confused and her body was aching, but the sight of Hector talking to her was surreal. He was so beautiful. For one moment, she could even forget she was hurting. But then she remembered she had been hit by something and sat up scared on the ground.

"You hit me!" she said, shocked. "Why did you do that?"

"It wasn't me. I was driving by, and I saw Kat hitting you on your bike. I just came here to help,"

"Did Kat do this to me?! Oh my, she is worse than I thought," she said in shock.

"I just broke up with her and I am glad I did it because she is totally crazy," he took a deep breath.

"What can I do for you? I mean, do you want me to take you to the hospital? I can drive you there,"

"No, I live close to here. I will call my dad," she said confused while still sitting on the road.

She reached for her phone and was shocked when she found a smashed screen.

"Oh, no. My bike is ruined and my phone too! There is blood on my shirt. I can't show up home like this!" Amalia said, starting to panic.

"Okay. Please don't panic. There is a cut on the top of your eyebrow, but it is a small one. So, let me move my truck closer and I will bring my first aid kit. I always have one in the car. Just don't move, I will be right back," he said trying to find a solution and comfort her at the same time.

Hector ran as fast as he could to his truck and moved it closer, behind her and her bike. He grabbed the first aid kit and ran towards her.

He asked if she could stand up and helped her to do so after she said she could. He got some gaze and medicine to put on a cut she had over her right eyebrow.

He carefully moved the portion of her hair covering her eyebrow and applied some medicine on it. Amalia grunted a little bit, while he covered it with a band aid. This moment, as trivial as it was, ended up becoming a deep moment neither of them expected. There were no words or sounds, but they couldn't stop staring into each other's eyes. It seemed they had become lost in each other's eyes.

Hector didn't know how to explain it, but he was controlling himself not to kiss her. Her long and dark hair blowing on her face, her lips, her expressive eyes, he never felt so attracted to someone as he felt for her.

Meanwhile, Amalia herself was trying to understand what was happening. It was Hector, who was in front of her, taking care of her. The most desired boy from her school, always so out of reach for her, and there he was with his beautiful smile, looking at her in a way nobody has ever done before. Was this real? What was happening? That was the only thing she could think of.

"Is it better?" Hector asked about the cut.

"Yes. Thank you," she said still in trance.

"Let me put the bike in the back of the truck, and I will take you home," he offered, and she nodded.

Usually, Amalia would never get into someone's truck - her dad's policy. "No car rides with boys." Her dad warned her, but she was hurt and being a little bit closer to Hector for a little bit more wouldn't be a big sacrifice.

He stopped the truck in front of her house, helped her out of the truck and took her bike out of the truck.

"Thank you. I don't want to bother you anymore, umm, you can go. Thanks again," she said, a little embarrassed.

"Let me take you to the door." he offered, and she accepted.

It was definitely a mess when she arrived home. Her parents ran to her worried, since there was blood on her shirt. They asked her what happened, and she said she had had an accident and Hector had helped her after it.

"Thank you so much for it. We don't even know how to thank you," Emilia, her mother said relieved.

"No worries. Is there a number I can call to check on her later?" he asked, wanting to talk more with her.

"I will give you my number and my email. I hope we can get another phone tonight" Amalia said as she didn't want to be without a phone, especially after what Kat had done to her.

"I can take you to the store if you want. My practice was cancelled" he offered, but her father interrupted.

"You have done enough, son. I will take her to the store."

"Sure. I will email you later then. I gotta go. I hope you feel better," he said, and he left the house afterwards.

Hector left the house absolutely intrigued. Why didn't Amalia tell the truth to her parents? Did Kat hit Amalia because of him, or because he broke up with her? Things were not adding up. Whatever was the reason, what Kat did to her was serious, and she could be severely injured or killed.

Why didn't Amalia think of reporting her? He should have told her he could testify if she needed to. Why didn't she let him take her to the hospital? She didn't fall from that bike but was hit by a car. She could have internal bleeding or something serious. All these questions occupied his mind one after another. The only thing for certain is he would rather be around Amalia and know more about her than be heading home. For Hector, the time they had together was not enough. He needed more.

He arrived home and parked the truck in the garage. He emailed her while still in the truck and she answered back, saying she was feeling better, but needed to rest. He wished her a good night and put the phone away.

He was getting his backpack to leave the truck when Jace called him because the game was about to start. With everything that happened, he totally forgot about it. He started the truck back and went to JC's home.

For Hector, it was good being around his friends. They talked about the game, had some snacks and drinks, but at halftime, they asked Hector if it was true that Kat and he had broken up.

"What's up with that? I thought you and Kat were doing fine. Kat is blowing in the wind she broke up with you, but we know it is not true. What's up? Mel said she was crying and everything," JC asked, intrigued.

Hector thought of saying what he had just witnessed that afternoon but didn't want to drag Amalia into that conversation.

"It was not real, period," Hector explained, without providing more details.

"And so what? Do you think Abby and I are for real? I mean we are together now, enjoying high school before life gets too serious, but we are not going to get married or anything like that. She is going to one school, and I am going to another one. We will be done. All you have to do is to lay low, man, go with the flow until high school ends and you will be a legend forever! No drama. Period!" Jace said as rational as always.

"Just for the record, Mel and I are for real. She is not a bad girl. She is just dragged by Abby and Kat. Okay, she is a little bit crazy, but I like her," JC explained.

"Well, good for you guys. I am not doing this anymore. I am done with that. The time I've spent with Kat were the three unhappy months of my life. So no," Hector said firmly, trying to end the conversation.

The game restarted, but Hector kept feeling uncomfortable at JC's and it had just become worse after the game ended, since his friends decided to have alcohol and smoke a joint.

"C'mon man, they are not testing us until the game. We will be clean by then." Jace tried to convince him.

"No man, I gotta go. See you tomorrow."

Hector left JC's and for the first time he felt like a fish out of the pond around his childhood friends. He made it home and went to bed thinking of Amalia.

Amalia looked at the stars through the window of her bedroom. While her body was still aching from the accident, earlier, she couldn't stop thinking of Hector and ended up sleeping thinking of him.

Hector & Amalia

Week One – Day Three - Wednesday

Boo!

Amalia arrived at school at the last minute. She stalled her father as much as she could for a series of reasons. First, she didn't want Little to pressure her to report Kat and her friends. Second, because every time she was in the school, she remembered how bad the chemistry test was, and third, she didn't want anyone to see the band aid above her eyebrow or the bruises on her arms and legs.

So, unlike the other days, instead of a bun, her hair was down. She had a cap on top of it to avoid any questions or comments and she was wearing long sleeves that day.

She spent the whole morning trying to avoid eye contact with Little. By her face, Amalia could tell Little wasn't happy at all. So at lunch, instead of going to the lunchroom, Amalia went to the library so she could hide there.

All she needed was a giant book she could hide behind. She went to the biography section and found a book about a designer she liked. The book seemed interesting and was gigantic, exactly what she needed.

When she moved the book, she had a surprise, since she saw Hector on the other side of the shelf. What were the odds of them being at the library at the same time?

"Boo!" She tried to scare him in a very gentle way. "What are you doing here?" she asked, whispering.

"Honestly, hiding from Kat. And you, hiding from Kat too?"

"No, I am hiding from Little, my friend," she confessed, embarrassed and they both laughed. He asked if she wanted to sit at the table in the back and she agreed.

The library was almost empty, and they ended up finding a table that was a little bit out of sight for the librarian and the front desk people. They sat in front of one another with their huge books in front of them.

"How are you feeling? I was worried about you. Did you go to the hospital last night?" he asked while pretending to look at his book.

"I am doing better, thank you. And no, I stayed home aching and missed Bingo at my church," she said, still pretending to read the book and he started to laugh.

"Bingo?! How old are you, ninety-five?" Hector said laughing. "What is there to like? The only time I played this was in my grand-grandpa nursing home, and I was ten I guess."

"Oh, there is a whole level of excitement in it, like football, you know? It is a thrill when you say 'Bingo!' and besides, I am fairly good at it! I always get the right cards and end up with a prize," she confessed, and Hector couldn't stop smiling. He asked her what prizes she got there.

"Well, I have a lifetime supply of Yankee Candles, fancy bar soaps, liquid soaps and my greatest prize was a tablet. Oh, and last month I got a toaster. See? I bet you don't get that at a football game,"

Amalia explained excitedly and Hector couldn't help but laugh.

"Yeah, nothing compared to a whole supply of Yankee Candles," he said while enjoying each second of that awkward conversation, and continued, "But I've gotten some magnets and a mug. So, it is something."

At some point their arms got tired and they put their books down. Their time talking gave him the courage he needed to ask some serious questions.

He asked her why she was hiding from Little. Amalia told him Little wanted her to do something, and she was not sure about it. She didn't want to upset her, but still didn't want to do it.

He surprised her, revealing some things about his friends.

"I know how it is. I feel the pressure. My friends and their girlfriends are always trying to push me to do things I don't want to, like drinking or other things. Sometimes they like to prank people, you know. I am usually strong enough to say no, but sometimes is hard," he paused and continued.

"There was this time when this house was empty, the owners were out on vacations, so my friends decided to go to the house and shoot the property with paintball paint, and I ended up doing some. I felt terrible afterwards," Hector admitted.

"Oh no! That was Meg's house. I remember that. Our church got together to clean it. It didn't come off, so they had to paint the house again. We had to do a fundraiser for it," she said disappointedly.

"Great! Now you think I am a terrible person!" he said embarrassed.

"No, I don't. I just think maybe you could talk to your friends about this, if they don't respect you, I don't know how good of friends they are for you."

"But you've said your friend Little is doing the same with you."

"No. It is not exactly the same. She is not trying to push me to do a bad thing. She wants the right thing to be done, but I am not sure if I want to do that. I had a pretty bad week too as I totaled the chemistry's test, and yesterday I had the bike incident, so, I just want this week to be over," she confessed.

"I feel the same. My English test was horrible. My dad is going to be really mad when he finds out about it, I broke up with Kat and then she did that with you…"

He paused and continued as he had realized something new.

"Wait a minute, is this situation with your friend related to what Kat did to you, isn't it? That's why she destroyed your phone. Well, that's a relief to me. I thought she did this to you because she was angry at me!" Hector sighed deeply.

"You are right. They are somewhat related. That's why she attacked me, and I didn't want to tell my dad about it. He would hire a lawyer or take me to the PD, and it is only six more months of high school to go, so no, I don't want this to happen."

"Well, I am with your dad on this, she could have killed you. But it is up to you."

They talked a little bit more and had the idea to talk to their teachers, literally begging for a second chance. If they got this opportunity, they could help one another with their respective subjects.

It wasn't easy, but both of them received their second chances. Their teachers would retake their tests after the Thanksgiving weekend. Technically they had the whole Thanksgiving break to study and improve their grades. That was the plan, spend the whole following week studying together to accomplish their goals.

Amalia

Week One – Day Three - Wednesday

After School

Amalia made it home and saw a note on the fridge. Her parents and brother were in the city next to her town to do some shopping since Rafael's birthday would be on the next day and Trendville certainly didn't have the brand stores Rafael liked.

Amalia couldn't help but smile when she saw the note. Her parents would rather leave a note on the fridge than text her cellphone. She held the note in her hands while thinking her parents were absolutely old-fashioned people.

She texted her mom, asking her to bring her a present so she could give it to Rafael and opened the fridge, looking for some of her mom's pastries. She heated one of them, poured some juice in a glass and ate some of it.

She couldn't stop thinking of Hector. What were the chances they would be in the library at the same time?

It was absolutely mind blowing seeing him behind the book she pulled from the shelf in the library. She fell asleep thinking of him the previous night, woke up thinking of him - his expressive eyes and his big and sincere smile - and there they were in the library at the same time. If she could, she would still be in the library talking to him.

She wanted to text or call him, but she didn't want to bother him or being too advanced, so she decided to do something that would calm her in times of stress - dance.

She opened her closet and found the two traditional Portuguese outfits her mother placed there. She took a deep breath and put the dress on. It is not that she didn't like it, in fact one of her best childhood memories was dancing traditional dances with her mom. Especially the one she was doing on Friday at Rafael's school, called "the vira" or "the turn" in English. It was a very rhythmical and precise style of dance, so she loved dancing it when she was a child. She liked it, but the idea of exposing herself publicly frightened her.

She went to the back of the house and put on Roberto Leal songs to play on her phone. He was a Portuguese singer her mother liked a lot in the 80's. She took a deep breath and started her practice. She was dancing and sweating when she heard a noise coming from the gate. She started to get worried since Kat could be back to hurt her, but she was relieved when she saw Little arriving in the backyard.

"What's up with you? It seems you saw a ghost!" Little asked and then she started laughing "Oh, my goodness, what dress is that? What are you doing?"

"Portuguese dance. There is a cultural fair at Rafa's school, and I am doing it this Friday so he can get two points in his next evaluation. Cool, isn't it?" she asked while she pressed a towel on her red and sweaty face.

"You are not helping your case. If people record this at Rafa's school, you will be mocked on social media in no time!" Little said worried.

"I know you dance at church, and you love it, but to dance at Rafa's school, in front of the whole city is a little bit much, don't you think? Tell Rafa to study. Period!"

"It is not that simple. You know my mom is struggling, right? She became so happy when I said I would do it, so I am taking one for the team," Amalia confessed. "Besides, I am invisible at school. Why would anyone care? I am sure they have other things to be worried about."

"Don't even tell me about it. Millions of people are living in poverty and hunger in the whole world and all they talk about is that H&K are not a couple anymore. Some say she dumped him, while others say the opposite. There are people devastated and in shock, because two high schoolers broke up! These people really need to get a life!" Little stressed and Amalia felt bothered by her comment. Would Hector rekindle with Kat? Better change subjects.

"I am done with my rehearsal, but before I need to tell you something," Amalia took a deep breath.

"I am going to send the video to your email so you can decide what to do with it. I decided I don't want to jeopardize Kat, Abby or Mel. They are wrong, but I don't wanna be the one who will prevent them from being accepted to college."

"Send me the video and I will have no problems with it. Time to execute some justice in that high school!" Little said, hugged Amalia and left.

After Little left, Amalia had a shower, put on a comfortable dress and laid down on her bed. Her mind was racing fast. She felt as if she was playing a chess game. Nothing was guaranteed at that point. The connection she felt with Hector could be true or not. Maybe it was all part of her imagination, maybe he was just being kind and polite, maybe this romantic feeling was solely coming from her. He could go back to Kat. They were such a beautiful couple. She was absolutely gorgeous with her shiny and long blond hair and grayish blue eyes. How could she ever compete with that?

And what about Little? Because she mentioned something to Kat, she hit her. Imagine what she could do to Little if she actually reported Kat and company? What about the chemistry test? How was she going to learn chemistry in one week?! All these questions were simply swirling in her mind after she showered.

She was thinking about those things when she received a text.

"Hey. I just finished practice now. I have some chemistry sheets to give you. Are you free?!" It was Hector. She smiled and said she was.

Hector arrived at her house five minutes later. Amalia invited him to the backyard since her parents were not at home. Hector was showered and wearing an old Beaver's shirt. While he seemed uncomfortable with his looks, Amalia thought he was even more beautiful in it.

When he decided to show up at Amalia's house, he was once again on the way to his own home. He was not usually impulsive, but all he wanted was to be around her, even if doing nothing. He felt as if there was a force pulling him in her direction.

He didn't have the time to go back home and dress up for her. He regretted it, after seeing how beautiful she was wearing a beautiful dress, with her long hair drying naturally, and that simple smell of regular shampoo and soap, even that was different on her.

"I hope you don't mind that we are sitting by the picnic table in the backyard. My folks aren't home, and my dad wouldn't want me being alone with a boy in the house, if you understand," Amalia said in a mix of embarrassment and excitement.

"Sure. I don't want to upset your dad, I can come another time."

"No. Stay. They won't take long to come back. It is okay."

Her eyes were so inviting, he couldn't say no.

"Let me just prepare something for us to eat so we can talk. You must be starving since we skipped lunch," Amalia said and he laughed, remembering how silly of them to be hiding from Kat and Little.

She heated some pastries her mother had cooked in the microwave and poured tea for herself and a bottle of sport drink for him. Rafael was also a player, and it was his favorite drink, so she thought he would like it too. They sat and she put the pastries on a plate for him and one for her.

"What is this? This is so good!" Hector said, eating nonstop.

"Portuguese sweet bread. I love this custard. It is one of my favorites," she paused a bit. "You haven't eaten anything since breakfast, right? That adds to the flavor!"

"I had a cereal bar before practice. That's all," he said and laughed at the situation.

What kind of date was this? What kind of first impression was he leaving on her, being there wearing an old shirt and eating all her food?

"I am glad I could feed our hungry athlete," she said and smiled. "Go Beavers!"

"People can never accuse you of not being supportive to your team," he said and smiled.

They were smiling at each other when her family arrived. It was absolutely an awkward situation when her parents and brothers arrived. They arrived with a lot of bags and her father didn't say a thing, but looked at both of them, as if he was trying to understand what was happening there.

"I came by to bring Amalia some chemistry sheets after practice and ended up staying longer. I think it's time to head home." Hector said, standing up a little nervous, getting ready to leave.

Amalia looked at her mother as if she begged her to do something. And she did.

"I am so glad you did this for her! Chemistry was never a favorite of mine, and knowing you came here to help, thank you for it." It was the best Emilia could come up with.

There was still an awkward atmosphere when Rafael finally raised his eyes from his phone and realized Hector was in his house.

"Oh my goodness, he is my favorite Beaver player! I always go to the game with my dad! Can I get a picture?!" Rafael asked excitedly and they snapped a picture together.

"Hey, my birthday is tomorrow. Do you think you can come at six? Please, come!" Rafael begged him.

Hector didn't know what to say and looked around before saying anything. On the one hand, Rafael was inviting him, but on the other hand, her father was not saying a word, as if he wasn't welcomed. Amalia looked at her father as if she wanted him to come and finally her mother put an end to the dilemma.

"It is going to be a homey and simple birthday party, but we would love it if you could come, right honey?" Emilia said and sought her husband's input.

"Yes. We will be glad to have you here." Ben said succinctly and Hector agreed to come.

"I will be here then."

Amalia followed him to the car, and they hugged before he left. They looked into each other's eyes and smiled. No words needed. Not that time. He climbed in his truck, waived at her and left.

She was going to bed when she received a text from Hector out of the blue.

"Can I call you Amy?" he asked, and she said he could, she asked how he would like her to call him.

"H." he said. "I enjoyed our time today. Good night, Amy,"

She received the text and smiled.

"Same here... Nice dreams, H."

She was still smiling while looking at her phone when her mother entered the room. She sat on her bed and started a conversation about Rafael's birthday, then ended up talking about Hector. She wanted to know what was going on between the two of them.

"Dad sent you here, didn't he?" Amalia asked and her mother nodded, smiling.

"I don't know yet, mom. I need some time with him in peace to find out. The only thing I know is it doesn't matter how much we talk; I always want more," Amalia confessed, and both smiled.

"Your father is concerned about you. He doesn't want to see you hurt, and Ben and his father definitely do not get along," Emilia said and took a deep breath. "What do you need to find out?"

"I think we need an opportunity to know each other in a calm environment, which is not school, for sure, and not with my dad and Rafa around. It is not that I want you guys to leave us completely alone, but we need some space," Amalia explained.

"What if you invited him earlier to the party tomorrow? Rafa has drama club tomorrow and I will ask your dad to wait for him there. Meanwhile you can show Hector the garden and the pavement you dance on. Just please, do not do anything that you shouldn't be doing," Emilia said a little bit nervous. Amalia laughed.

"I will not betray your trust, mom. I promise. And thank you."

Amalia

Week One – Day Four - Thursday

Family Tradition

It was Rafael's birthday, and Amalia's family had a tradition of spoiling the person on their birthday, which meant doing things they were never allowed to do or eating what they were not usually allowed to eat. They tried to do this this year, but Rafael was really going overboard.

"What? Pizza, ice cream and chocolate for breakfast?! Never!" Emilia was outraged.

"It is his birthday, mom," Amalia helped Rafael, which was not very usual for her.

"Ok. But one slice of pizza, one scoop of ice cream and a small piece of chocolate."

"Deal!" Rafael said and winked at his sister.

For what they all knew of Rafael, that would be a *long, long* day for all of them.

At the Larkin's, while Amalia finished breakfast with her family, Hector was eating a bagel with cream cheese in the kitchen and having some coffee with his father after another excruciating morning in the gym.

His father told him his mother was ordering Italian food that night for dinner and Hector needed to text his mother what he wanted to eat so she could order.

"Tell mom to not wait for me. I will be late for dinner."

"Third time this week, H. We barely see you anymore. If you have a date with Kat, you can bring her too. Your mom likes her."

He would really like to tell his father they were not dating anymore, but if he said this, he was sure his father would drop dozens of questions on him - His father would not like the answer, and he didn't want to bring Amalia in it since it was too early for him to risk ruining what they had.

"It's a friend's birthday, dad. The game will be tomorrow. We can see each other after the game," Hector suggested.

"Okay, but we are fishing on Saturday. I already told Matt, James and Dave, you are going,"

Drew told Hector about the fishing plans, and he could feel his jaw contract. Matt was JC's father; James was Kat's father and Dave was Jace's father. He definitely didn't want to go but knew he had no other choice.

He entered his car in the garage and received a text from Amalia.

"Good morning, H.," she wrote, and he smiled.

"Good morning, Amy. Hiding in the library today?" he asked, curious.

"Little and I are fine. No reason to hide anymore. Sorry. You can sit with us if you want," she offered and he was very tempted to accept, but whatever they had was too early and vulnerable to face all the pressure at school.

"I guess I will sit with Clay and Pat today, but I will be there for Rafa's birthday," he answered finally.

"If you want to come earlier, you can," she texted, and he smiled. He was going to see her earlier. That was definitely good news.

It was lunchtime at school and Amalia saw Hector and his friends sitting at a table on the *haves* side of the lunchroom. She looked at his table in a discreet way and saw him talking and laughing with his friends while eating. She couldn't explain but he looked even more handsome than he did on the day before and seemed not to have noticed her presence yet.

Little called her attention since they were in the line, and it was her turn. Amalia was absolutely absent-minded. Finally, their table was fixed and back in place, no more disagreements in order to have a place to eat.

They sat and they started talking about the morning classes. The art teacher said their evaluation would be a group work. A documentary to be delivered after Thanksgiving. They were struggling to find a theme for his documentary.

"Don't you come with Shakespeare, please! I want something fresh and real, something that would actually stand out in some alternative movie's competition, not only for school, but for real producing companies," Alfred announced his ambitious plans.

"You must have bumped your head this morning. How are you going to compete with people all over the nation in your first movie?" Little asked, being realistic.

"Well, I don't have a theme, but I believe in you. If you want a dance movie, I'm in." Amalia suggested it and smiled.

"Maybe a worship dancing documentary." Alfred said and continued.

"We could film you dancing with your hair flying in the air. That's not a bad idea. Let me see the length of your hair," Alfred said while he stood up and went behind her seat.

Alfred took her hair tie off, dismantling her usual bun and touched on it, checking on its length and texture. Amalia didn't care because Alfred was like a brother to her.

The four of them have been friends since third grade. He touched her hair and did some movements on it, pretending it was moving in the air.

Amalia was smiling and amusing herself with the idea, it seemed meaningful and fun. She would love to create a movie about worship dance and spread the idea as much as she could. And as Little would say, she was not afraid to make a fool of herself.

She was smiling while Alfred played with her hair and suddenly, she crossed looks with Hector. He was looking at her and didn't look happy seeing Alfred touching her hair.

"Enough with my hair, please. You already saw me dancing in the church. So, think about it and let me know if I am hired," Amalia said, trying to make it lightly.

"Ok. I will definitely think about it," he finalized.

She looked back when they were leaving the lunchroom, and her eyes met with Hector. They smiled discreetly to each other, and she went back with her friends to her class.

Hector & Amalia

Week One – Day Four - Thursday

Rafael's Birthday

Amalia put on one of her comfortable dresses. Yes, it was fall, but it was also the South. While they would have some days in which they would feel like fall, this week wasn't one of them. It was not hot either, but comfortable enough she could wear one of her relaxing and comfortable dresses.

It was exactly 4:30 pm when Hector arrived at her house. Seeing him brought an instant smile to her face. He was not wearing an old t-shirt like the day before. He was dressed up, wearing a quart sleeve shirt and jeans. She concluded it was impossible to resist him.

"Hey stranger. Are you ready to work? I need to collect some flowers in the garden," Amalia invited him.

"Sure, I brought this for Rafa," he said pointing to a bag.

"Let me put this inside and we will go to the garden."

Amalia left the bag inside the house and told her mother they were going to the garden to collect some flowers for Rafael's birthday. They winked at each other because Amalia was definitely putting the plan in place, to know more about Hector.

She showed Hector the garden her father had set aside for her. He saw all the herbs, spices, plants and flowers she had proudly planted herself. He had to pretend he was really paying attention to what she was saying, because all he could think about was how she looked beautiful in her colorful dress and the smell of soap and shampoo exhaling from her while she talked and walked around the garden.

"Oh, I almost forgot, I have a surprise for you!" she said with her eyes sparkling.

She got a basket with a blanket and some snacks, a bottle of sport drink and water, so they could sit on the blanket and talk.

They set up the blanket and sat next to each other. He started to drink the sport drink she gave him, and she started to drink water while they talked. They talked about the second chance the teachers have given each of them and tried to set up a plan to study during the holiday week to prepare for the test.

While she talked, Hector started to be unsure of how long he could wait to kiss her. He didn't want to be too advanced but couldn't wait any longer.

"I don't know how to say this, but, umm, can I kiss you?" he finally had the courage to ask because it was the only thing he could think about.

"I am not going to kiss you if you are not my boyfriend," she said, feeling her heart beating fast.

"Do you want to be my girlfriend?

"Yes," she said nervously, and he kissed her.

They kissed and when they did it, it seemed they were both transported to a place they had never been before. A place where things have a different pace, where a second could last a lifetime. A place deeply filled with peace and love.

"I wanted to do this since the first time I saw you," he admitted, smiling. Still trying to process everything he was feeling at the moment.

"I know it was only a couple days ago, but it seems like it took forever." Amalia also admitted and touched his face. "Are you sure about us being together?"

"One hundred percent. No doubt about it," he said, pulling her close to him and touching her hair.

He had dreamt of having her this close to him, and then that's exactly where she was, in his arms. The feeling of peace he had when he was around her was new to him, something he had never experienced in his life.

There was no doubt his parents loved him, but there was always a lot of pressure over him. Being around her, it took him to a place where he never wanted to leave. It was not her house, or the farm environment, but herself. Somehow, she could bring him this feeling of peace and quiet.

Suddenly Hector felt comfortable enough to tell her about his dreams of becoming an NFL player. He was ready to fight for it, even if it meant going against his father. He explained to her that football was the only thing he saw himself doing in the future.

He also shared with her that there would be a scout to see him in the next game and he hoped to get his attention. It was senior year, his last opportunity to win the championship, winning it could help him in the future.

Amalia listened to him carefully. She never thought he was such a deep person, so confident, with so many plans laid out for the future. He asked about her plans for the future, and she felt embarrassed, because she was nothing like him.

She said she was set to go to a Christian college close to their town, not a big and well-known school but a school with a good design program. She hoped she would find herself in it.

They were talking when her mother called on her phone saying Rafael would arrive in 30 minutes. They definitely had to go back to the house.

Amalia decided Rafa's birthday would be in the backyard since the weather was good and it wouldn't rain, according to the online forecast.

She covered the table and placed the flowers in the little vases on the table. The cups used to be old jars and were transformed by Amalia's crafts. She placed the plates and napkins on the table. Her mother put the homemade cake in the center, and she also brought some Portuguese pastries, including Rafa's favorite, called in Portuguese, pastel de Belem, which looked like a mini pie dough filled with an amazing custard. All they had to do was leave the space on the table to bring in the pizzas, Rafa's favorite too.

Rafael and his father arrived, and they all hugged him and congratulated him on his birthday. He was definitely blushing. Hector took one wrapped present from the bag, kept it, and gave the bag to Rafael. Inside there was an official Beaver plush toy with the Football team logo embroidered and an official jersey.

"Wow! That's the best gift ever! Thank you!" Rafael couldn't be more excited. "Thank you, mom for the cake and the party; thank you, dad, for the gifts and thank you, Amalia for dancing the Portuguese dance tomorrow at school. I really appreciate that!"

"Are you dancing tomorrow? I didn't know this," Hector said, surprised.

"Oh, I thought she had told you. She is going to be the first one to dance tomorrow at four at my school and she will be wearing a traditional outfit. It is free. Anyone can come!" Rafael said with a big smile on his face.

After Rafael told Hector about her presentation, all Amalia's compassion towards his birthday was absolutely gone. All she wanted was to place a piece of duct tape over his mouth.

Ben said a prayer for Rafael, they sang Happy Birthday (Amalia started just because Rafael hated it) and afterwards they ate and drank, Rafael asked

Hector to throw some football with him. Amalia said he couldn't refuse since it was Rafael's birthday, and he did.

They left the table to play a little bit, close to the cotton field while Ben, Emilia and Amalia watched them having fun. Both of her parents looked at her, as they expected her to say something about Hector.

"Please don't freak out, but we are dating. We are happy and sooner or later he will talk to you guys," Amalia announced and saw her mother smiling, while her father was definitely trying to process the fact his little girl had grown and was actually dating someone.

Time went by fast and before they realized, it was nine in the evening. Hector would have to wake up at five to go to the gym the next day and he would have an important game in the evening too.

Before he left the house, Hector turned to Ben a little bit nervous.

"Is it okay if I date your daughter?" he asked, knowing Ben expected him to do that. Ben looked around hesitantly and said.

"Yes, it is. Just take care of her," he asked.

"I will."

Amalia followed Hector to his car, and he gave her the package he was holding the whole time. It was his team's jersey, and it seemed to fit her perfectly. She put it over her dress, not caring if the dress matched the jersey or not.

"You are so beautiful in it," he said and pulled her by her waist and kissed her on her lips.

"Go Beavers!" she said, and they smiled. "Thank you! I am not sure yet, but I will try to be in the game tomorrow."

"I hope to see you there!" he said and got in his truck. "Oh by the way, I hate sports drinks."

"Sorry, I should have asked,"

She said and smiled, feeling bad for him, remembering how many of them he had because of her.

"It's okay. I just couldn't drink another one," he said and smiled at her before leaving her parking place.

Hector

Week One – Day Four -Thursday

After Rafael's Birthday

Hector arrived home, and he still felt as if he was floating in the clouds. He couldn't believe they were actually dating. Amalia's kisses were even better than what he thought, as were her hugs and the touch of her skin when she held his hands.

He walked in through the garage door and found not only the living room lights on, but also his father was sitting in his armchair, wearing his pajamas and robe. He was never downstairs at that time. Hector knew his father was waiting for him.

"Hey dad."

"I just learned today you and James' daughter broke up. Why didn't you tell me?" his father asked straightforwardly as usual.

"I didn't think it was a big deal. It is my dating life, so I didn't think it would matter," he said, knowing that wouldn't be the case.

"You are wrong about that. Her father is my business partner, and yes, it matters to me I didn't know you were not dating his daughter anymore." Drew took a deep breath.

"You are right, it is your dating life, but if you met another girl, please do not take her tomorrow to the game. Give it some time, ok?" his father asked him, and, surprisingly, Hector agreed with him.

As much as he wanted Amalia to be at his game the next day, maybe it wouldn't be a good idea, since his breakup with Kat had happened recently.

"Okay."

Before sleeping, Hector texted Amalia and said he would rather her to go to the following game. He explained it was too early for them to go public and also there would be a scout at the game. He needed to focus on playing well. She agreed and said she would go to the game after thanksgiving.

"Good night, H."

"Good night, Amy."

Hector & Amalia

Week One – Day Five – Friday

Early Morning Thoughts

Amalia woke up filled with many emotions. Yes, on the one hand she couldn't be happier as she was in love and they were dating, but on the other hand, things were still not settled. There was so much to talk about, and they didn't have the opportunity to do so.

She looked at her phone and realized she had woken up much earlier than she usually did - Partly from excitement and partly from concernment. She knew the days at school would be awkward from that moment on.

School had always been the place where she had to deal with people like Kat, Mel and Abby. It had been uncomfortable before, and it was worse since Kat hit her in the beginning of the week and she was also Hector's ex-girlfriend.

What still lightened her days at school were her friends. But even these moments with her friends became awkward since they didn't know anything about Hector, not even Little knew about him. She was around them but with this overwhelming feeling she was hiding something big from them.

Hector, she thought, was in the same awkward position. He could no longer hang out with his longtime friends since the two of them dated Kat's besties and he had no other options but to hang out with other players during lunchtime.

But in spite of the awkwardness, and the worst for her, it was not being able to be around him, holding hands, like any other couple. All they could do was to enjoy one single moment where their eyes were going to meet.

They didn't have the time to have a proper talk about their situation at school, but it was as if they had it. They knew it was not the time to expose what they had together. Amalia could only imagine Little's shock when she found out she was dating a *haves* one. It would be the same with Hector's friends.

She sighed discouraged and remembered it was the cultural fair and Hector's game day. She prayed for him and the scout who would be in the game that night.

"Do the best for H., Lord," she asked while starting to fix her backpack.

She heard a beep in the front pocket of her backpack.

"Do you want a ride?" It was Hector. "Game day. Kinda nervous. Need to see you."

She smiled after reading it. All she needed was to be with him, even if it was for a minute.

It wasn't easy for Amalia to convince her father to allow Hector to drive her to school. Ben finally accepted but only after Hector promised he would take good care of her. They finally got in the truck.

"How are you doing?" she asked, and he didn't hold back.

"Freaking out," he said, honestly. "Between the game, the scout, my dad, Kat, and not being able to be with you in public, I'm not great," he said, as she touched his right arm, to comfort him.

"I haven't talked to Little yet about us, H. I plan to do it this evening," she announced.

"Okay. I'm thinking about it, you know, how I am going to tell everyone,"

He stopped the car on the way, so they could talk calmly.

"I missed you," he said, and they kissed calmly.

"Me too," she said in a sweet tone of voice.

Her father texted Amalia asking if she had arrived at school. They looked at each other and smiled. Ben would always find a way to track them. They knew it was time to go on their way to school.

"You can drop me behind the library. Nobody will see," she said as soon they arrived in the back of the building.

"I hate this," he confessed.

"Me too," she said, shrugging her shoulders. "I will be praying for the game," she said leaving the truck.

Amalia

Week One – Day Five - Friday

Cultural Fair

Amalia arrived 20 minutes before her presentation at Rafael's school and her mother was waiting for her. They had a room behind the stage where she could change clothes. The short amount of time she had to dress, she spent asking herself how she agreed to do that since she remembered seeing a lot of cars in the parking lot.

Her mother helped to fix her hair as soon as she was dressed. She looked at her mother terrified, and her mother whispered in her right ear.

"Dance like those days we used to dance in the backyard... You will always be my favorite dancer." Emilia said touched and Amalia felt her eyes getting full of tears and emotions.

The host of the event announced the name of the Portuguese dance and said the piece would be performed by Amalia de Souza. Amalia took the stage and waited for the song to begin. When the song started, she started to dance, and suddenly, she couldn't see their faces anymore. She could only see herself and her mother dancing and laughing in the backyard.

The frenetic movements were followed by all the joy she remembered from her childhood, of simply doing something fun with the person she loved the most. It all went by so fast Amalia couldn't believe it. When she realized, they were all clapping and cheering.

When Amalia left the stage, her mother, brother, father, Little, Alfred and Alex were all there, waiting to congratulate her.

"You all came!" Amalia said, surprised.

"We would never let you be embarrassed alone, never!" Little said hugging her.

"Are we going to the ice cream place or not?" Alfred asked.

"Ice cream is on us today!" Ben announced.

Amalia couldn't see, but Hector was there in the back. He recorded her dancing and was going to talk to her when he saw all her friends showing up to congratulate her, so he didn't. He heard a buzz on his phone. Coach Jonhson wanted to see him. He had to go back to school. The game would start at seven and he wanted to talk to him about some strategies for the game.

Hector

Week One – Day Five – Friday

Game night.

While Hector was waiting to talk to coach Johnson, he couldn't stop thinking about the game they were going to play in a few hours. They had not beaten this team in the last 3 years he had been in high school. And they needed to defeat this team in order to continue in the championship.

This game could mean a scholarship to the school Hector wanted to attend or not. A scholarship carried by his own efforts, not something his dad gave him.

This game could mean the possibility of bringing the championship to Cotton County after twenty plus years or not. Definitely, there was a lot on the line in this game.

"H. Come in and close the door!" Coach Johnson called him. Hector entered the room and sat in the chair in front of him and he went straight to the point.

"First of all, the scout is coming tonight, he called me. Second of all, I don't want any trouble with your father, so, if this has a positive outcome, leave me out of it."

"Ok. Is that it?"

"No. I have some good and bad news. I'll start with the bad ones. One of the referees is going to be replaced tonight and the guy who is replacing him canceled a touchdown and took a couple points from us before. So, it may happen *again.*" Coach Johson said.

"I need you to have cold blood, H. You are the captain. If you lose it, the others will too."

"I remember that guy. How is he still a referee?" Hector asked in disbelief.

"I don't know. I know myself and other coaches complained about him, but nothing was done," he saw Hector shaking his head and continued.

"You know what it means. You need to be prepared to work double or triple to win the game."

"That's great!" Hector said sarcastically.

"But here comes the good news. Have you seen Adam kicking the goal before? He scored ten out of ten, H. If you can take the ball to Adam in the right place, he will not miss it." Coach Johnson revealed it to him. Hector liked the idea, but he knew it wouldn't be easy.

"If we can pass through the guys, it is a great idea."

"I know, their players are stronger and taller than ours, so I will need Clay, Jace and JC to deal with the rough guys, getting the ball and passing it on to you." Coach Johnson said and continued.

"You need you to make the ball get to Adam. If we can do that, we can win."

"If JC, Jace or Clay are able to get the ball from those guys, I will take the ball to Adam." Hector promised.

"Awesome. So let's go to the room. I need to talk to the other players. If we pass this team today, we will really have a chance to win this championship."

Amalia

Week One – Day Five – Friday

Coffee Time

After ice cream, Amalia invited Little to go shopping downtown. They would have only about 40 minutes left before the stores closed. They went to a few stores, and she asked Little to go to the bookstore before they headed home. Amalia wanted to be home by seven to watch the football game broadcast.

The town's only bookstore was charming and had a small coffee shop located in the back. They both ordered some coffee and started sipping on it when Amalia finally told her about Hector.

"So, I am dating someone," she said, and Little looked at her intrigued, as if she was asking who the person was.

"Hector," Amalia said, a little nervous.

"Larkin?! Are you joking? That guy is an idiot. Meg's neighbor is sure it was his truck which left her house the night Meg's house was vandalized," she said, absolutely shocked.

"He is a good person, Little. You are going to like him with the time," Amalia defended him.

"Is this a prank? You gotta be kidding," Little said in shock, trying to process everything.

"The "haves" people have been treating us like garbage all these years, how can you date one of them?! What are you going to do now? Are you going to be friends with Mel and Abby too? The girls who bullied us our whole life?! They are Hector's friends. You will have to be around them, you know that, don't you?!"

"I know it is hard for you to understand, but he is not like them," Amalia pleaded.

"Maybe this is all what it is - a prank. He is probably using you and then will discard you in a few months from now, just so he can make fun of you and us to everyone. Yes, that's it."

"Can you stop with that?!" Amalia protested.

"Why aren't you going to the game to support him? Did he ask you, by any chance, not to go to the game? Have you already met his family? Has he met your family? How come you don't get together at school if you guys are dating? Is he hiding you from everyone? Why is he doing this? Is it because he is playing with you, or because he is embarrassed to be with a *have not*?" Little started to ask so many questions Amalia started to get a headache.

"It is complicated," it was the only thing Amalia could say.

"No, it is not. He is messing up with your feelings and I am going to prove it to you!" she said beyond furious.

After Little's outburst, Amalia said she was not feeling well and wanted to go home. Little drove her home; they were both in silence on the way. When they reached Amalia's house, she asked Little not to say anything to anyone.

"I won't, but I will prove to you he is lying," her last sentence before she left Amalia's house.

The game was about to start, but Amalia could not watch it. She was so torn about how she felt about Hector and all those questions Little brought up. She was even physically feeling sick. She felt as if she could vomit any time with how bad she was feeling. Would Hector have the courage to use her? Was he hiding her because he was embarrassed of her? Why did he ask her to not go to the game? She turned off the light and went to sleep, crying.

Amalia woke up hours later, with a buzz in her phone. She thought it was Hector, sending a text message, but it wasn't. It was Little.

"I wish I was wrong." The text sent by Little followed by a picture of Hector and Kat together with the headline, "Are they going back together?"

Amalia's heart sank with this news. She cried for some time and then decided for what calmed her the most: Dance to God. She started to dance on the pavement her dad built for her behind the house, in front of the cotton field.

Hector

Week One – Day Five - Friday

A Celebration Dinner

Hector, his father, mother, and Kyle, his 10-year-old brother, arrived at the local country club's restaurant. It was one of the most expensive and fine restaurants in Trendville. There were several tables joined, and there were only four spots left at the table, precisely for Hector's family.

As soon as Hector and his family arrived at the restaurant, they were greeted and cheered due to the Beaver's victory. A remarkably tight game with the final score 38-35.

"I knew you would win, that's why I reserved these tables for all of us! I knew this would happen." Jace's father said enthusiastically.

Hector laughed to himself. They were so close to losing that game. He had to admit his friend's father had a lot of faith.

They sat at the table, and he immediately wanted to run away, since Kat was sitting very close to him. Matt, Jace's father, asked his son about the most important parts of the game, and Hector couldn't avoid laughing. Jace always had a funny way of saying things.

"You have no idea. There we were Clay, JC and I trying to fight those giant and humongous guys, actually. So I said to JC 'Man, we are smaller, but we have to get this ball.' The guys looked like rocks, we had to pile up on one of them to be able to tip the ball from the guy's arms," he said, and Hector started laughing because it was fun to see Jace, Clay and JC trying to fight those huge guys over and over again, trying to get the ball.

"Thinking back, I suspect those guys were not 17," JC said suspiciously.

"Yeah, and all that work for the referee to call back our first touchdown. Man, I was angry. All that hassle for nothing!" Jace remembered.

"And what about Adam? He fired two touchdowns, crossing routes. I couldn't believe it!" Hector confessed, impressed.

For a moment, Hector forgot everything and had a good time with his old friends Jace and JC. Kat was at the table, but luckily, she was on the opposite end with her mom, dad and sister. They were laughing, talking and eating appetizers, when suddenly, Matt asked Drew about a mall project they had.

"De Souza ruined it again. You should have seen the council meeting, it was ridiculous! That guy was even able to persuade the girl we put there on the council to vote against us. Can you believe this?!" Drew asked, beyond upset.

"That guy is ridiculous. We would be ten times richer if it wasn't for him," Matt said frustrated.

"But keep the project on standby, it is going to happen sooner or later. Meg is getting old and none of her kids will work on the land, not even De Souza's kids will either. Do you really think his kids want a hard farm life? He will end up selling it too," Matt talked about their plans and Hector started to feel nauseated with the conversation.

"I saw them yesterday" Marty, Jace's mom said with a polite tone of voice.

"They were all in middle school. It was the cultural fair, and I was volunteering there. His daughter was dancing, I guess a Portuguese dance. What is her name again? Amelia? Something like that. She has really grown, and she reminds me of her mother when she was young." she added with her polite tone of voice and fine manners.

"Who? *Amalia Old Phone?*" Jace asked, mocking her and Hector could feel his stomach revolving. Jace kept going.

"Apple has launched iPhone 100, and she still doesn't have the first iPhone. I would be embarrassed to talk to people on a trashy phone like that."

"Jace!" his mother reprimanded him.

"He is right, Marty. The girl can't even buy a decent phone because her father is ruining this town. If he let us build the mall, she could get a job and a new phone and wouldn't have to be living in poverty," Drew said and that was the last straw to Hector.

Hector left the table and said he was going to the patio in the back of the restaurant as the main dishes hadn't arrived at their table. He felt so miserable he could not explain. He knew his father didn't get along with Amalia's father, but the hate he heard coming from his father's mouth was real. They were laughing at his Amy! They were making fun of her. They would never accept their relationship. His breathing became heavy.

"Are you okay?" It was Kat who went after him. "I was concerned about the way you left the table."

He looked at her and could only remember how she hit Amalia on the bicycle that week and left her on the road as if she were something disposable.

"Tired. It was good to see you, but I have to go," he said and went back to the restaurant.

Hector made it home and went to his bedroom. He was still hungry and texted his mother to bring him something from the restaurant. He checked his phone and no messages from Amalia. Not a single one. As much as he missed her, the things he heard that night about her made him feel unsure to the point he started to question himself if they should be together. He had a shower, changed clothes, and went to sleep.

Hector

Week One – Day Six – Saturday

Early Morning

Hector woke up early since his father wanted to fish with his friends. He looked at his phone twice. There were no messages from Amalia. He watched her video dancing again at the Cultural Fair. Her vivid smile, her frenetic movements, her sparkly eyes. That video reminded him of other things about her - The shampoo smell in her hair, the connection they had when they kissed for the first time.

Maybe it was better to end this way. He thought. But just the thought of her not being a part of his life made everything feel gray, tasteless, and numb.

"Good morning, Amy." He ended up sending a message but had no response.

His father knocked on his door saying he was waiting for him. It was definitely time to go.

Amalia

Week One – Day Six – Saturday

Trying to Keep it Up

It was eight thirty in the morning when Amalia woke up. At the De Souza's house, breakfast was always late on Saturdays. Her father knocked on the door, and told her breakfast was ready. She sat on her bed and saw Hector's message, and as much as she wanted to answer, she didn't. After all the questions Little placed in her mind and after the photo she saw of Hector and Kat, she needed to put things on pause until she had some answers. No matter how hard they were.

She sat at the table for breakfast and all her father and brother did was talk about the game. The Beavers won in the final minutes, defeated their biggest rival, and now advanced to the championship. Every time they mentioned the game, the team or the players, it was like someone was punching her in the gut over and over again.

"Have you talked to H. today? When you do, tell him we are proud of him," Rafael said, all proud of his future brother-in-law, but Amalia's mother knew her well enough to know she wasn't fine.

"Can you talk about anything other than this game?" Emilia asked and placed her eyes on Amalia, giving a hint to her husband Amalia wasn't well.

"Rafa, let's go to the market together. I guess your mom needs some things." Ben invited him so he could leave Amalia alone.

"Can I have an ice cream at Meg's?" Rafael's answer to the invitation.

"Again?!" Ben took a deep breath. "Okay. Let's go."

Amalia finished breakfast and went back to bed. Emilia was so concerned with her that she called Little and asked her to call Amalia.

Little called in no time asking if Alex could be there in the afternoon so they could define a dance choreography for the art documentary.

Amalia was still sad but the perspective of spending her day doing nothing, remembering the picture of Hector and Kat wasn't the best alternative.

Alex arrived at her house after lunchtime. He brought his boombox and his tablet for the school art project. This would be their exam. They needed to plan the choreography, and practice the moves, so they could decide what they would keep or not. Amalia was waiting for him wearing a gym top, leggings, and a t-shirt on the top of them.

Alex put on a gospel rap he liked and thought it would be interesting for them to dance and she liked the idea. Alex talked so much about games and videos he watched, they usually forgot how good he was at dancing. He started to show her the moves he had thought for the dance and Amalia started to follow him.

"One-two-three-four, turn around and go down," he said, showing her.

Amalia was trying hard, but there was one of the moves she was not making properly, and he came up behind her, held her hand and showed her the movement her arm and shoulder should make.

"Argh! This is so hard!" she said, frustrated.

"Ok. Let me teach you one more time," he said and got closer to her in order to teach her the same step.

Since she was so focused on getting on track with the choreography, Amalia didn't hear her mother's voice. All she saw was Hector standing in the backyard looking at her.

Hector & Amalia

Week One – Day Six – Saturday

A Serious Talk

As soon as Amalia saw Hector in the backyard staring at them, she stopped dancing with Alex and moved his hands away. It was an awkward situation; one they didn't know what to do or say.

"Tried to call you like 10 times. Now I know why you are not picking up," Hector finally said and turned his back to leave.

"H., no! Don't go, please. I forgot my phone inside the house, and we need to talk," she pleaded with him to stay.

Hector turned back to her and got closer to her and Alex. Alex, poor Alex, he looked very, very confused. He couldn't understand why Hector and Amalia were looking so serious to one another.

"What's going on here?" Alex asked, trying to understand.

"Exactly, what is going on here?" Hector asked and Amalia decided it was time to end practice.

Amalia told Alex they could continue practicing on Monday. She offered to take him to the door, but he told her he knew the way.

Alex left and Hector still looked upset. She told Hector she was going to take a quick shower so they could talk calmly.

She stepped in the shower, and it was her time to be upset with him. How did Hector dare be upset with her when he himself was the center of the school gossip pages on social media? He had no right to be.

She left the house and went to the backyard to talk to him. Her hair was still wet, while she was wearing one of her comfortable dresses.

"I tried to call you before coming," he said, hurt.

She looked at her phone and saw he tried to call her several times, saw the selfies he sent her while fishing with his father and saw his texts asking if he could come by at the end of the day. He finally said he would come by as soon as he came back from the river.

"Sorry. I didn't see your texts," she said, trying to initiate a conversation.

"What's up with you and your friends? Every time I see you around them, there is always someone touching you and touching your hair," Hector inquired.

"First of all, we were rehearsing the choreography for the art documentary. Second, Alfred and Alex are like brothers to me. So, it is not a big deal."

"I am risking everything for you, and you don't even remember I exist! I have been texting you, calling you, and sending you pictures, and you just didn't even care to check your phone," he said, upset.

"How is Kat, H.? Was she fishing with you today?!" She showed him the picture of the two of them and Hector was in shock.

"She is much worse than what I thought. I went to the patio of the restaurant last night because they were making comments I didn't want to hear. She showed up there, I spent like 10 seconds with her and left. And now there is a picture of us together, as if we were going to go back?!" he asked, trying to understand who would do this, and then he thought about Amalia.

"Did you think this was true?! Is that why you didn't want to talk to me?" he asked, and she nodded.

"I am sorry, Amy. This is far from true."

"It seemed very real to me," she confessed.

Hector and Amalia went to the place they were before. They sat together on the blanket and held hands. Amalia explained to him about the documentary they were putting together for the art class, and he shared with her that they were doing a documentary about football, of course. They exchanged ideas and suddenly Amalia asked.

"What were they talking about for you to leave the table? Were they talking about us?" she asked and after taking a deep breath, he nodded.

"Were they talking badly about my family during the dinner?!" Amalia asked in shock.

He stood up from the blanket and she did the same.

"That's why I left. And the truth is nobody is a saint here. Do you think I don't know what people say about the *haves*? For you guys, we are arrogant, greedy, snobbish, cruel, and heartless, and this couldn't be further from the truth," he said defending his family and friends.

"Sorry, but that's not that far from the truth. What about Meg's house you guys damaged? What about Kat trying to literally kill me to destroy my phone?" Amalia confronted him.

"You can't judge a whole group of people for a few. Do you have any idea how many people my father has helped? He donated all our uniforms, all of them. Last year, a boy got hurt on the field and my dad paid his hospital bill because he didn't have the money to do it! My mom? Oh, my mom and her friends, they do so much charity in this town you have no idea. They help the churches, people in need. I wouldn't be surprised if some of these Yankee Candles were donated by them," he said, trying to defend his part of the town.

"Well, I didn't know that. Sorry," she said, sincerely, and tried to change topics. "I didn't know you were jealous either."

"Neither did I. This is new for me. I had tons of girlfriends before, and it never bothered me when someone touched or hugged them. With you it is different," he confessed.

"I missed you," she said, getting closer to him and they ended up hugging and kissing.

Sometime later, Hector and Amalia were laying down and talking calmly on the blanket.

"This is going to be harder than I thought. My father hates your father. I've never seen my father talking like that about anyone. I was so upset. I wanted to defend your father, but it seemed the words didn't come out from my mouth," admitted Hector.

"I know. I feel the same. Little had the same reaction when I told her I was dating you. I never saw her like that. I tried to defend you, but she wouldn't listen. It was terrible," she confessed.

"We need to be united. We need to communicate better. We need to trust God, you know? It is the only way we are going to survive it all," he said while holding one of her hands.

Week Two

Worlds In Harmony

Amalia

Week Two – Day One – Monday

Hope in Trendville

It was eight in the morning when Amalia got up. She intended to sleep a little bit more since they were off school that week, but her phone didn't stop buzzing. There was an email from the art teacher telling them the art project was postponed and she felt relieved.

Amalia also got notifications from her social media account. Little had posted a reel of her dancing *Bless the Lord* from Matt Redman at the church the day before and many people liked the video and also encouraged her for the upcoming worship dancing competition that will take place by the end of the year.

The outpouring of love, encouragement from the people of her church and the good news from school was a great way to start her morning. She only felt sad because Hector couldn't be there since he went to another church, in the rich part of the town. They had agreed to wait one more week before disclosing their relationship at school. One more week and they would be able to be together at church.

She left the bedroom and found out her mom had prepared her some breakfast and set aside a part of the table for her and Rafael.

"I am going to have some more coffee so we can talk!" her mother told her excitedly.

They started to talk about many subjects, from the dancing competition to her performance at church on the morning before, to her relationship with Hector.

She told Amalia she met her father when he came to visit relatives in Portugal. At first, she didn't even consider looking at him because she didn't want to leave her family behind in Portugal, but given time, Ben started to conquer her. His patience and decency made her feelings grow more and more. They started dating a day before he left for the US, but they were in love and determined to be together. It took them two years to finally be together, but they did it and were united until the present day.

This wasn't the first time her mother mentioned her love story with her father, but this time, Amalia was in love and their story resonated in a different way to her. If her parents could face an ocean and two continents to be together, there was hope for her and Hector in Trendville.

Hector & Amalia

Week Two – Day One – Monday

Afternoon in the Attic

Hector arrived in the afternoon at Amalia's and was relieved to know practice with Alex had been cancelled since the art project had been postponed. It meant they would have the whole afternoon to be together. He brought the chemistry books and Amalia called him to go to her dad's man cave. A neat attic in which her father used to store his treasures. They found the Bob Dylan records from her father, kept in the attic all those years.

While they were listening to some of the songs and talking about them, Hector asked if he could snoop at some of the photo albums. He was surprised to find a whole album of Ben de Souza and his father playing on the same team. They were always together in the pictures and were always smiling, side-by-side, like many of the pictures he had taken with Jace and JC in the last years.

Hector was shocked to find this out. His father always talked about the golden days when he played football in high school but had never mentioned he and Ben were friends in the past. It was as if Ben De Souza had never existed in his father's life.

"Did you know our fathers were friends?" Hector asked, shocked.

"Yes. My mom told me about it. They were great friends until they parted ways,"

"Do you know what happened?" he asked, curiously.

He asked, and Amalia was very tempted to tell him what she knew. Amalia's mother told her they were friends until Drew became greedy and betrayed their friendship with Ben, who at the time had just been appointed for the first time as a councilman.

Ben De Souza trusted Drew Larkin would build homes for the low-income people from the town. That was the agreement. Drew was his friend, he wouldn't lie to him, right? After the upscale mansions started to be built, people started to question Ben's capabilities to run the city council. De Souza's morale was so low he decided to take a trip to Portugal, to visit family he had never met, that's when he ended up meeting his future wife.

But Amalia couldn't tell him this. It was not her place to tell, especially when she knew how much Hector loved and admired his father.

"Maybe one day you can ask your father about it. Don't you want to see my children's pictures? Let me show you some," she asked, changing subjects.

Amalia opened an old album and started looking at the pictures with Hector, they were seeing the pictures of when she was four years old, and Hector was surprised. He was in one of the pictures side-by-side with her. How could it be?

They had never been in the same class. They went immediately to ask her mother about it.

"I am as surprised as you are," Emilia said marveled while they were looking at her waiting for answers.

"But I know who could give you the answers you want, Mrs. Andrews! She just came back from New Jersey. I met her yesterday after church." Emilia remembered.

Hector and Amalia looked at each other. They had to talk to that teacher, maybe she could remember something about that picture.

Emilia called Mrs. Andrews and asked if she could help Amalia to solve a mystery from kindergarten and she agreed to meet with them.

Before they could even realize, they found themselves sitting on Mrs. Andrews couch, waiting for her to tell them what she could remember from that picture.

"Aww. I remember that day as if it was today. Amalia's teacher got sick, and they split her class between the two other kindergarten classes while her teacher was in recovery. Amalia was so scared to be in a new class, she cried every day. I didn't know what to do with her anymore,"

She took a sip of her sweet tea and continued the story.

"One day, you, Hector, got out of your seat and told her to stop crying because you were going to protect her, and she stopped crying. She believed in you, and you were always around her until her teacher returned," Mrs. Andrews got emotional remembering it.

"Wow! That's crazy!" Hector said in shock because he still had the same desire to protect her.

"Time flies for sure... I took this picture when we received news the teacher was returning. I wanted to keep a picture of the kids with me before they left, and I gave one copy to Emilia," she paused briefly and asked, "Are the two of you together?"

"We are not telling anyone yet, but we are," Amalia confessed to her.

"Aww, it is so good to see the two of you together again. It is like going back in time."

They left her house, and they got in the truck overwhelmed by the discovery of that afternoon. While they held that picture, they felt this strong connection, a feeling they were always meant to be.

Hector & Amalia

Week Two – Day One – Monday

A Bittersweet Call

After solving their childhood mystery at Mrs. Andrews house, Hector dropped Amalia at her house and went home.

He was in his bedroom listening to Bob Dylan songs and reading about them when the phone rang. It was Coach Johnson. When Hector saw the coach was calling him, his heart started beating fast since the phone call could be about the scholarship.

Hector picked up the call and Coach Johnson said he had good and bad news.

"The bad ones first. Please," he asked nervously.

Coach Johnson said he received a phone call from the scout asking him to see Adam's footage, not his.

Each word coming from Coach Johnson was like a punch in his gut because Hector knew exactly how things worked. If the scout was asking for Adam's footage it was because his teammate had captured their attention, not him.

Hector was so disheartened he couldn't say a word during that phone call. Coach Johnson knew him enough to know how disappointed he should be.

"H.? Please, let me tell you the good news," he said, breaking the silence.

Coach Johnson told him there was another scout in the previous game from another university who had contacted him, asking for Hector's footage.

He went on saying the school had a great football program, some of their students were actually playing professionally, some of them had been drafted by the NFL and the scout seemed very interested in him.

"He said they want more than a player, H. They are looking for a leader. I know you are both,"

Hector was still upset, but Coach Johnson words not only comforted him, but also encouraged him.

"One drawback only, H. They want to see a resume with charity and community work you are involved in. They are a Christian college and do a lot of outreach in their community. They said this is important for them. So, I hope you can think of something really quick to add to your resume."

"Sure. I will think of something." Hector finally said.

Hector ended the call and had mixed feelings. First things first, he could not believe after all the work he put in, the coach asked for Adam's footage instead. This was beyond frustrating.

All his plans were laid out. He would get the scholarship, he would fight to build an NFL career and graduate at a school which had a great program of Business Administration, exactly like his father desired for him. So, he would do what he wanted without fighting his father. But again, the scholarship would probably go to Adam.

He called Amalia to vent about the situation.

"I am sorry, H. I know it is frustrating for you, but I have been praying for God to do the best for you. And even if we can't understand it, we need to trust this is His will for you," she said, trying to comfort him.

"Sure. It is easy to say this when you didn't work for it! If I kicked like Adam, I would have gotten it!" he said, frustrated.

"H., please don't do this. Adam's family are struggling financially for so long. They would never have the resources to send him to a school like this. I wish there were two scholarships. You both work so hard, you both deserve it."

Amalia said honestly and tried to focus on the positive news.

"But, what about this other University? Maybe it will be better since you want a career in the NFL."

"Well, it doesn't hurt to check."

"We are going to have a fall festival in our church this Wednesday. We wanted to do it before, but we didn't have the funds for it. You could help the kids play on the inflatables. Also, pastor James does his visitations at the hospital on Friday. You could join him. What do you think?!" Amalia asked, trying to help him.

"Not a bad idea." he said, while his mother called him to have dinner. "I gotta go. Dinner time. Good night, Amy,"

"Good night, H.,"

Amalia

Week two – Day Two – Tuesday

Unanswered Knocks

Amalia woke up early and saw her father working in the fields through the kitchen window. He hired Jeff, one of the neighbor's kids to help him on the farm.

She sat at the table where they usually ate and saw a note from her father.

"Mom is not well today. Please be patient."

Amalia held the note in her hands and her heart started beating fast. She was so immersed in her relationship with Hector she didn't realize her mother had gone to bed early the night before.

She remembered the note her father left and knew what it meant, her mother was probably in a melancholic state of depression, and they had to make things happen until her mother was feeling better again.

Amalia put the coffee pot on, made some scrambled eggs, cooked some bacon, toasted a couple slices of bread, and set the table. When she finished it all, she texted her father and he came into the house to eat. Rafael was still sleeping, so they could talk openly about things. They talked a little bit about the crop, ate some, then she asked how her mother was doing.

"I don't know. She was crying when I went to bed, there was an album in the room. Not sure if it is related to how she is," he answered her, and as soon as he mentioned the album, she knew what had happened.

"Oh dad, this is all my fault. I took the album to her because I wanted to ask about a picture, but the album was probably full of grandma's pictures. If I hadn't taken the album to her, she would be fine," she said, feeling guilty.

"No Pumpkin, it is not your fault. Mom has tried to hold it together for a long time. It is Thanksgiving week, which is even harder for her," her father told Amalia, trying to comfort her, but he continued talking, since she wasn't getting any better.

"Mom always did everything for us, right? Now it is our turn to help her. I am going to take this food to Jeff, you cheer up and we will talk later, ok?" he asked, and she finally nodded.

Ben went back to the cottonfield, while Amalia washed the dishes. She left Rafael's plate covered on the table and started looking for something she could cook for lunch. Pasta, tuna and sauce was all she could find quick and easy to make.

Since her mother was diagnosed with depression the previous year, she had to adapt to these days. Days in which it seemed no one or nothing mattered to her mom. It was like she was traveling, but she wasn't. Her mother was right there in her bedroom, but unreachable. Amalia knocked on her door a couple times, but she had no answer.

Hector & Amalia

Week Two – Day Two - Tuesday

Teamwork Afternoon

Amalia was lost in her thoughts when she saw Hector parking his truck in front of the house. Her mother's situation had made her forget he was coming by later in the morning. She opened the door, they kissed, but he realized she was not well.

He asked what was going on and she told him her mother had been battling depression since her grandmother passed away the previous year, and she was not well that day. He took a deep breath when he heard it all.

"Look, I know your mom is not well, ok? But I don't want you to ruin the chemistry test because of it. You fought for this chance to redo the test, and I don't want you to miss it,"

"I know but I need to cook lunch now, wash the dishes and the pans," she said discouraged.

"So, we can cook together and go somewhere to study, what do you think?" Hector suggested.

Ben showed up at the house and woke Rafael so he could eat breakfast before it was lunch time. Her father was happy to see Hector around since Amalia really needed some support that day.

Ben told Amalia he had to go to the hardware store, the bank and other places, but he would try to be back as quickly as possible. Rafael said he hated tuna and begged his father to bring him a cheeseburger from a burger place in the city nearby. Ben and Emilia were not fans of fast food, but he decided to make an exception.

"Well, isn't it your lucky day?! I have some business to deal with in the city so I can do this today. Ask your sister the wi-fi password and no more than one hour," he said before leaving.

"And, do I have to tell you anything, Pumpkin?" Ben asked, obviously referring to the two of them in the house.

"No dad, I already know," she answered embarrassed.

Hector being with her at the end of the morning helped her to cheer up. They found a recipe on the internet and started to work on it together.

"It can't be that difficult," he concluded while preparing to cut the onions.

A couple seconds later he was crying while cutting the onions, and Amalia couldn't stop laughing.

"You knew it, didn't you? That's why you asked me to cut the onions specifically." he said, noting how she was amused with his *onion's tears*.

"Sorry, I just couldn't resist," she admitted smiling.

They finished preparing the pasta and set up the table for the two of them. Rafael was not joining them since he was saving his appetite for his fast-food sandwich.

Amalia knocked on her mom's bedroom door and asked if she wanted to join them, but she didn't hear an answer.

"I will leave some in the fridge for you," she said and went back to the table.

Amalia looked discouraged and sad. Hector didn't know what to do to make her feel better until he went to the bathroom and saw a Yankee Candle in the vanity.

"So, I was thinking, if you improve in chemistry after lunch, I could take you to the bingo tonight," he offered, knowing this would make her feel better.

"The church bingo?!" she asked with her eyes sparkling. "Aren't you going to feel embarrassed?"

"Absolutely, I am going to burn some bridges after that, but it can't be worse that cutting onions."

Hector and Amalia studied for the chemistry test after lunch. From the 10 questions, Amalia got eight rights, so he felt she was making progress. They agreed he would pick her up for the bingo at ten to seven, but asked what he could do before leaving.

"Can you run the dishwasher while I do some laundry?" she asked while taking the basket to the laundry room and he agreed. She had just put the first load in the washer when she heard him calling her name.

"Amy, can you come here, please? I guess there is something I didn't do quite right," he said almost in a desperate tone of voice.

She hurried to the kitchen, and she was in shock when she saw what was going on. There was soap everywhere. Like, everywhere.

"Goodness, what have you done? What soap did you use?!" she asked in absolute shock.

"This one," he said, holding the little bottle of liquid dish soap close to the sink.

"Oh my, in what world do you live in? This one is *the* dishwasher soap!" she said pointing to the bag, filled with the dishwasher tablets.

She was so in shock she started to laugh and couldn't stop it anymore.

"So, you are telling me this was your first time running a dishwasher in your life?!" she asked, and he nodded, like a guilty five-year-old boy caught doing something wrong.

"Oh H., you are such royalty..." She was still in shock.

"You will remember this forever, won't you?" he asked, already knowing the answer.

"You bet I will," she said in a mixture of shock and laughter.

Amalia told Hector it was better he went home before her father arrived and saw that mess. He still felt guilty, but she assured him she would take care of it, and he finally left.

Hector left and she looked at all that mess. She had to hurry up before her father arrives home.

Hector & Amalia

Week Two – Day Two -Tuesday

Bingo Night

It was 6:50 pm when Hector arrived to pick her up to go to the church bingo. Amalia had a pair of jeans, a blouse with polka dots and a huge bow close to her neck. She didn't want to tell him, but that blouse was her mother's when she was young. For a minute, she was concerned with how it looked, but Hector's sparkling eyes towards her buried her insecurities once and for all.

Amalia left home excited to go to the church bingo with Hector. She had also invited Little to go with them, since they hadn't opened their relationship yet. They got their bingo cards. Hector got three cards for each of them and paid for them while Amalia looked at the prizes, trying to figure out the one she desired the most.

Amalia saw a journaling kit which would be perfect for her Bible verses journaling she used to do with her mom. But that night was definitely not a good night. She couldn't win on any of the cards she had with her, which had never happened before.

"Lucky in love, bad luck at games. It seems you can't have it all," Little said, being provocative.

"I can't say this. I am winning everything! It seems this game was made for me!" Hector said excitedly and Amalia felt they had joined forces to remind her of her "bad bingo" night.

On the way back, after they left Little at home, Amalia couldn't pretend she was happy. She hadn't won a single card, Hector won two prizes, and he was boasting about them the whole trip. She was boiling inside.

"Can you stop with that, please?" she asked in a bad mood.

"Oh, what happened with 'I am an artist; I am not competitive and there is a place for everyone?'" Hector provoked her with her own words.

"Can you *not* say anything until I get home, please?" she asked, upset.

They arrived at her house, and he gave her a bag before he left. She opened the bag when she entered the house and saw the journal kit she wanted so much in it with a note.

"Let's say I had to swap a couple prizes to get that. H."

Amalia headed to her mother's bedroom and her door was still closed.

"I got something for you. I know you will like it. I will leave it here at the door," she said and went to her bedroom.

She entered her bedroom, laid down on her bed and started to think about everything she had experienced with Hector that night. His excitement every time he matched a number on his card.

Looking back, even having Little and him plotting against her was nice to see. It gave her hope one day they could all be friends and coexist in peace.

And the cherry on the top was Hector giving up on his prizes to give her the one she wanted. She decided to message him before going to sleep.

"Sorry for being grumpy on the way home."

"Good to know you can be competitive too. That makes me like you even more," he said, and she smiled.

"Good night, H."

"Good night, Amy."

Amalia

Week Two – Day Three - Wednesday

Red, Orange, Yellow and Green Preparations

Amalia woke up and remembered it was the day before Thanksgiving. It didn't feel like Thanksgiving or sounded like Thanksgiving. With her mother locked in the room and the absence of her grandmother, it really didn't seem like it either.

Thanksgiving week had always been big in their home. Her mother and grandmother worked together the whole week so they would have plenty of food, the house would be sparkling clean, the smell of cinnamon and pumpkin spice in the air, and the red, orange, green and yellow decorations would be all around. But with her grandma's absence and her mother's reclusion, it all felt too bland and ordinary.

If it depended on Amalia, nothing would be done. But she couldn't stop thinking of Rafael, her 11-

years-old brother who always enjoyed the season and the food. He surely would miss it.

"So dad, how is it going to be? I know mom is not okay, but I don't want to miss the whole holiday." Amalia started the conversation during breakfast.

"What's on your mind?"

"I could make some boxed pumpkin cookies and cake. You could buy a pumpkin pie at the store and a whole dinner maybe, so we wouldn't have to do it?" she suggested and smiled.

"You mean one of those dinner combos with everything ready?" he asked, and she nodded. "Okay. We can try that."

Ben de Souza left to take care of usual business and Amalia started to scrape some decorations from the previous years in the garage. She didn't take long to find the containers since they were clear ones, and she started to sort things out.

She opened the container and found the wreath her grandmother made, the hot pads for food she knitted specially for Thanksgiving, the napkins she sewed and also the napkin holders made specially for the occasion. Her grandma was present in every bit of that container, as she used to fill her house with her discreet and loving presence.

After looking at the container, Amalia knew she would need to do something different this year. Her mom was already devastated and having memories of her grandma in every corner of the house wouldn't help. Amalia called Little and they left for downtown. Before she left, she opened the money jar her mom kept for emergencies, and according to Amalia, this was an emergency. She grabbed $40 out of it and went to shop with Little.

Amalia bought a patterned fabric to sew them a new tablecloth and some solid-colored quarters to make different napkins. She also purchased some seasonal flowers which were on sale to create a centerpiece for the table, along with lots of disposable plates and napkins.

"Wow! You are really going wild!" Little said laughing, remembering Ben and Emilia hated spending money on disposable things that wouldn't last.

"It is an emergency! And I don't want to wash all those dishes afterwards," she said, revealing the real reason.

Amalia and Little arrived home, placed the begs on the top of the table, grabbed her own small sewing machine she had had since she was a kid and started working on the tablecloth.

Forty minutes later, it was done. - the tablecloth and the napkins. Little also suggested creating a banner with the fabric leftovers and this time they opted for gluing it all. They high fived each other after they saw the final result. The Thanksgiving mission was definitely accomplished.

Hector & Amalia

Week Two – Day Three - Wednesday

Fall Festival and Ice Cream

It was four in the afternoon when Hector arrived at the house to pick her up as the fall festival was scheduled to start at five pm. They also picked Adam on the way. Amalia was dressed as a farm girl and Adam and hector were dressed as football players.

As soon as they arrived at the church, they went their separate ways. Hector and Adam left for the inflatables and Amalia and Little went to the games area. Little was at the Cornhole game and Amalia was face painting the kids. The festival started and it seemed like the whole town came to enjoy it. They worked hard and they were almost done when Little spotted a toddler running towards the road.

"Get the kid! Someone get this kid!" Little yelled and Hector jumped off the inflatable and ran as fast as he could to reach the boy just in time.

They were all tense, but Hector was able to catch the boy on time. Everyone started laughing because he got back holding the boy as if he would hold a football. At the end, they all ended up having ice cream at Meg's Bakery/Ice Cream Shop.

Alfred, Little, Adam, Hector and Amalia were having ice cream when Alfred said he had a very scary thing to show Amalia. He showed her a picture on his cellphone, and she said she was terrified of the image. Hector couldn't understand and Alfred showed him the picture of a yellow parking cone. He saw the picture and seemed all put off by it.

"Can you guys stop telling him all my secrets, please? Ok, the truth is I am terrified of yellow cones. They are the reason I haven't driven a car until today! That's it!" she confessed it.

"Why?" Hector asked, confused.

"It is because she hits all the cones in the driving test instead of avoiding them," Alfred spilled the beans.

"You are joking," Hector said, shocked.

"No, I am not. Every time I take the test, I freak out and hit all the cones in front of me. I have done the test three times already. I am starting to think I am destined to be a bike rider," she said laughing at herself.

Hector had to control himself to not kiss Amalia, or to not touch her hair, or to not kiss her while she was laughing and talking with her friends, but he couldn't since nobody, except Little and Adam, knew about them. Being around her and not being able to hold her was a kind of torture. So he had an idea and asked Adam to help him with it.

Hector & Amalia

Week Two – Day Three - Wednesday

Hayride Under the Stars

They left Meg's shop and Amalia was sure they were going back home. Adam had the keys from the church, and he said he had forgotten something on the way.

They left the truck and went back to the church instead.

"I have a surprise for you. Come with me," Hector said, holding one of her hands.

Amalia followed him to the back of the church property but had no idea what he was talking about.

At that point Adam was nowhere to be found and the lights of the church building were out, which made so many stars show up in the sky.

Adam showed up out of nowhere, driving a small truck with a hayride wagon on the back of the

174

truck. It was then Amalia realized the place Hector took her was the place hayrides were happening earlier that day.

Adam drove the truck to the place Amalia and Hector were. He left the truck, came to the back of the truck and opened the wagon chain, which would allow them to go in.

"Mam, Sir, you can climb on the wagon. Our trip is about to start." Adam said, still dressed in his football jersey.

They climbed the wagon and found a place to sit on the back of the wagon. They sat on the wagon floor and supported their backs in a block of hay. There was hay everywhere, even on the floor they were sitting on.

Adam went back to the truck and turned the engine on.

During all her life, Amalia had been in so many hayrides, but none like this. While the truck started to move, Amalia and Hector were holding hands, feeling embraced by the wind around them and the sparkle coming from the lights in the sky.

While the wind was blowing Amalia's hair, Hector pulled her closer to him, holding her. They were in silence, living the moment. They looked and smiled at each other while they could feel the truck move around the property.

Amalia was so attracted to Hector, to his beautiful smile and he was even more beautiful wearing his football jersey. Her long hair was floating in the air and even in a farm jumpsuit and plaid shirt, Hector couldn't stop looking at her, enjoying every moment he could have her so close to him.

Time flew by and the ride was over before they could realize, but Hector and Amalia knew they would never forget their first hayride together under the stars.

Hector

Week Two – Day Four - Thursday

Thanksgiving Morning

Hector woke up and could feel the buzz going on in the house. The sounds of steps and voices. People coming and going, being busy, doing all sorts of things around the house. He opened his bedroom door and saw the catering and the cleaning people moving around. The ones his mother had hired to provide her family and guests with an impeccable house and food.

Thanksgiving at the Larkin's was more than a family tradition and celebration. It is also a day his father talks business to his guests, makes new alliances and solidifies old ones. The mayor and his wife confirmed their family's presence at the event and his father was very excited about it. For Drew Larkin, Ben De Souza always found a way to keep him on a leash and cut his wings, but he knew if he could bring the mayor to his side, some changes could happen in the town.

Thanksgiving at the Larkin's was an event. Better to say, *the* event. The most prominent people from the town would surely be there. Thanksgiving was the day Jace, JC, Kat, Abby and Mel pretended to be good boys and girls. They would dress up in a conservative way, have impeccable language and would be on their best behavior. Hector took a deep breath. The day would be a long, long day.

He went to the kitchen and there was a catered breakfast for the family and the workers too. There were donuts, bagels, grits, juice and coffee. Year- after- year, it happened the same. Hector grabbed one of the mugs, put it on the coffee maker, waiting for the coffee to pour in his mug.

"Finally I see you. So, I was thinking we could have lunch together away from this craziness. What do you think?" his father suggested.

Hector would love to get out of the house, but he promised Amalia he would have lunch with her family. The De Souza's changed their celebration time so Hector could participate, and as far as he knew, Amalia's mom was still not okay. So, he couldn't miss it.

"I can't, dad. I promised this girl I am seeing that I will have lunch with her today. I already gave her my word, so I can't," he explained.

"Well, if Kat weren't here tonight, you could invite her."

Hector felt the palms of his hands sweat when his father said this. If his father saw him arriving with Amalia, De Souza's daughter, at the party, the world would probably end.

"I know dad, but as you said, Kat will be here tonight, and it is too soon." he said it referring to Amalia.

"Humm, I don't know about that, H. I have barely seen you this week. What is her name? Why the mystery?" inquired his father.

"Okay. I promise I will bring her here next week," Hector said while feeling a knot in his throat. "I give you my word."

"Okay. I am counting on that." Drew finally said.

Hector & Amalia

Week Two - Day Four - Thursday

De Souza's Thanksgiving

While Hector was having breakfast with his father in the kitchen with the constant passing of people, Amalia was also having breakfast with her father. Rafael was sleeping. Her mother was still in her bedroom and Amalia was only waiting for breakfast to be over, so they could move on with the day's preparations.

"She ate something and showered last night. So, it is a beginning," Ben said about Emilia.

"Do you think she will be here for lunch?" she asked, confused.

"I hope so," Ben paused a little and continued, "Thank you for stepping up. I know it is taking longer this time, but mom will be better, ok? Just give a little bit of time,"

"Okay,"

As soon breakfast was over, Amalia knew she had no time to waste. She prepared the cookie batter in one bowl, took Rafael out of bed and made him place the cookie dough in the cookie sheets. While the cookies were baking, she was preparing the batter for the fluffy pumpkin cake her grandmother used to bake every year.

She took the cookie sheets out and placed the cake batter in the oven. That's when she started to decorate the house by placing the new tablecloth on the table along with the plates, napkins, cutlery and a vase with the clearance flowers on the center of the table. She also placed the cups on the table and remembered two of her Yankee Candles. One was Pumpkin Spice scented and the other one, a Cinnamon scented candle. The Pumpkin Spice was lit on the top of the fireplace mantle and the Cinnamon one was placed in the bathroom with the red hand wash towel in there.

Rafael helped her to hang the Thanksgiving banner on the top of the cupboard behind the table. The cake smelled good from the oven. She took it out, and all she had to do was to wait for her father to come with the rest of the meal.

She had a shower and tried to find something different to wear, since Hector had seen her in the majority of her dresses. She just wanted to surprise him. She took a deep breath and knocked on her mother's bedroom door, saying she needed a different dress.

"Are you upset with me?" her mother asked when she was leaving the room.

"A little. Grandma is gone, but I am not," Amalia said trying to hold back her tears and left the room.

Ben arrived at the house with the Thanksgiving meal he ordered from the grocery store and the pumpkin pie. Everything smelled good. Hector arrived with some donuts and bagels he had snuck from his house, and they all sat to eat. Lunch was about to start.

"Is there space for one more?" Emilia asked, standing in the kitchen.

"Sure! Please sit here with me!" Ben's face lit up when he saw her all showered and dressed up.

"You did an amazing job! Everything is so beautiful!" Emilia said, amazed at the result.

Ben said a prayer and they all started eating. The meal ordered from the store was surprisingly good and they all had a good time eating, talking and laughing.

Having Emilia and Hector at the table with them, eating, drinking and celebrating was definitely Amalia's reason for giving thanks.

The lunch and the early part of the afternoon was so pleasant Hector didn't want to leave. Everything was so cozy and homey, he felt so comfortable and relaxed, but when his father started to text him, he knew it was time to go. He said goodbye and left Amalia's house. Thanksgiving was just beginning for him.

Hector

Week Two – Day Four -Thursday

Thanksgiving Dinner at the Larkin's.

Hector was getting ready for the party when his father entered his room. While he continued dressing up, Drew asked him to be more present in the conversations he was having during the evening. This is because all his business in Trendville would be Hector's one day.

His father explained having Hector, the captain of the High School football team, next to him would help him with new business deals. When his father finished talking, Hector knew he had to take one for the family.

The night was longer and worse than Hector imagined. Several times he caught Jace, JC, Kat, Mel and Abby rolling their eyes begging to go home, so they could stop pretending they were *angels* and go back to their own lives.

It was so awkward, Hector had lived around them his entire life, but suddenly he felt so disconnected it was hard to explain. He couldn't stop thinking of Amalia dressing in her flower-patterned dress. She was so naturally feminine. The smell of the house, the coziness and the laughs at the table. Everything was so organic, so natural, so different from what he was used to in his own home.

He was thinking about it when his father called him to talk to the mayor. They talked a little bit about football, how the team was going and talked about the chances of winning the championship. Everything was bearable until his father started talking about business.

"I've heard the farmers petitioned the city hall for loans so they can invest in their lands. I know you want to see some progress in Trendville. What if you vetoed this funding? Don't you think it could help the city to grow?" Drew asked in a very natural way and Hector felt sick to his stomach.

His father was trying to jeopardize people's families. Including the families of Little, Amalia, Alfred and Adam. He definitely didn't want to be part of that.

"I don't think I should be here in this conversation," Hector said, visibly bothered.

"No, you stay. You have to learn because one day you will be doing this," his father said, and Hector knew he had no option but to stay. Drew turned to the mayor then, "What do you think about what I said?"

"I sure want to see some progress in Trendville, Mr. Larkin, but I can't do this. I was elected because I am a neutral person who moved here two years ago. Half of the city who voted for me are *have nots*, as you call here. If I veto De Souza's petition, I will surely lose my job." he said confidently.

Hector was relieved when the mayor didn't take part in his father's plot against the farmers, and even more relieved when the last guest left. His feet were sore from standing up for so long in dressed up shoes, and his cheeks were aching from smiling all night long.

His father was excited because once again he had made new connections and partnerships. Hector went to his room and didn't take long to fall asleep thinking of Amalia and the great time they had earlier that day.

Amalia

Week Two – Day Five - Friday

Girls Time

Amalia woke up with her mother knocking on the door. She opened the door concerned, but her mother seemed much better than the previous days.

"I thought we could go out to Nancy's shop to get some stickers and start Bible journaling together. What do you think?"

"I think it is amazing!" Amalia said, jumping up from her bed.

That morning was a special one for her mother and her, since they had a lot of fun finding different stickers and colored pens. They started writing down the Bible verses which inspired them the most. They wrote a couple of verses and decorated the pages. It was fun and also a big relief since Amalia's mom was much better.

They sat to have some ice cream at Meg's when her mother apologized for her absence, for not being well and for Amalia having to keep the house going even when she couldn't.

"It is hard to see you in that state, mom. But you know, we are so used to dropping everything on you that we failed to recognize that you also needed help," Amalia took a deep breath.

"Truth is, we can do more. Me, dad and Rafa. I know grandma is gone, but you have us. You can count on us,"

Amalia said and they both were touched by the conversation. They were leaving the store and getting in the car when Hector called and said he needed to see her before going to the hospital visitation with Adam.

"I thought you were in the hospital already," she said, surprised.

"I can't do this. I am freaking out." he was hyperventilating.

"What am I going to say? What am I going to do? What if I say the wrong thing and the person gets worse?" Hector was desperate and Amalia was shaking her head, trying not to laugh at his desperation.

"H., you are unbelievable! So, you are not afraid of having a bunch of guys jumping on you, hitting you or hurting you on a field, but you are afraid of visiting people in the hospital?!" she asked in disbelief.

"Yes! I am! I am freaking out!" he confessed, and she looked at her mom. Her mom whispered she would take Amalia there.

"I'll meet you in front of the hospital".

Hector & Amalia

Week Two - Day Five - Friday

Hospital Visitation

Amalia arrived at the hospital and Hector was sweating as he didn't know what to do. She hugged him as soon she entered his truck, and her smile brought him some peace. For a moment he was able to forget his fears and concerns.

"Let's pray for God to give you wisdom and use you to spread His love," she invited him, and they prayed together.

She promised him she would go into the rooms with them and take pictures if they wanted. It was a way to show him support and help with what they needed.

Amalia was with them when Adam and Hector entered the hospital. They were representing the high school football team and wearing the football jerseys. Everyone was excited about having them there. They were also invited to go to the hospital children's section, and seeing the kids' faces beam when they saw them, it was special for her to see this.

Hector took some little gifts for the patients and snapped pictures with the ones who wanted them. Amalia brought a polaroid from her mom's car, so the picture was printed immediately. One photo for the patient and one for Hector and Adam for a keepsake.

They left the hospital, and they dropped Adam at his dad's farm. Hector stopped the car on the road and started to sob nonstop. Amalia was there with him trying to understand what was going on.

"That little boy had not eaten anything since yesterday, but he decided to eat because we told him to," he said and couldn't stop crying. "They were so happy when they saw us there."

"I saw it. It was beautiful. I was touched by it," she confessed.

"How come you didn't cry?" Hector asked.

"Oh H., I have done this since I was 15 with Pastor James' team. At first, I was very emotional, but with time you learn to enjoy the moment and brighten someone else's day," she explained.

"The kids used to love when I juggled," she said very naturally, and Hector could not believe what she said.

"Juggled? Juggled what? Like the people in the circus?!" he asked and started to laugh, wondering if it was real or not.

"Yes. Like the people of the circus. My dad took me to the circus when I was what, eight, I guess, and I became totally obsessed about it. Every day I watched juggling videos on YouTube, and I became fairly good at it," she said, and he started laughing.

"You are kidding me?!"

"No, I am not. I still have my full juggling set. The circles, the balls and the pins. The whole thing," she said, feeling goofy for amusing him.

Amalia's juggling expertise changed the tone of the conversation, and he couldn't stop laughing at her juggling memories. It was a great way to end the afternoon.

Hector & Amalia

Week Two - Day Five - Friday

A Fancy Dinner

The afternoon went fast, and Hector invited Amalia to celebrate their one-week anniversary at a restaurant in the city nearby. He asked her father's permission, who reluctantly accepted and allowed Amalia to go with him. Hector and Amalia crossed the Trendville border, since they didn't want to be seen together yet.

They arrived at a fancy restaurant his father used to take his mother to a couple times. The riverfront restaurant was so refined and sophisticated in a way Amalia had never seen before.

"What are we doing here? I am not dressed for this place!" she said looking down at one of her mom's dresses she was wearing from the nighties.

She said wanting desperately to leave, while Hector amused himself with her concerns.

"You are cute, and this dress is fine," he tried to assure her that she was dressed according to the place when she saw the menu.

"Oh my goodness, we can't pay for this!! We are going to jail!" she exclaimed in shock, and he couldn't stop laughing at her reaction.

"It's okay. I'll just spend a third of the money I had saved for college, but it is fine."

"No! You won't. We are leaving now!" she said whispering while standing up to leave the restaurant.

"Sit down, I am joking! My dad gives me an allowance, but I never spend it on anything, so we are fine, I promise you. Now can you relax, please?!" he insisted.

The dishes arrived. Amalia ordered a tuna medallion, mushroom and salad, while Hector ordered some steak, fries and green beans. They were eating and talking while Amalia realized some people were looking at them and making some comments. She asked Hector while they were looking.

"They probably think we don't have the money to pay the bill since we are young," he said, and Amalia had to agree with him.

The way the servers and waiters were looking at them reminded her of what they would have to face the following week at school.

"Are you sure we are ready to go public at school on Monday?" she asked him, trying to make sure they were on the same page.

"Oh yeah. I can't stand not going to church together or not being able to hold hands in public. I'm done with that. I am sure, Monday is the day,"

Hector dropped Amalia off at home. She smiled when she saw her father waiting for her on the porch, and he rarely went to the porch. Ben and Hector greeted each other, and he left.

Amalia had a shower and prepared to go to bed when she saw Hector's text

"Busy day tomorrow with my family. Fishing with my dad's friends and their children during the day and a birthday party in the evening. Thank you for this week. Can't wait for Monday."

Amalia read his text and smiled.

"You make it hard not loving you. Love you. Good night, H.," she said, shaking, while she wrote the text.

The "l" world was big and serious. Should she have done this? She thought while she realized it was too late to take it back. Five minutes passed and no answer from Hector. Five more minutes and a text came back.

"You make it impossible not to love you. Love you. Good night, Amy."

"Good night, H.,"

Week Three

Worlds on Fire

Hector & Amalia

Week Three – Day One – Monday

Facing *Haves* and *Have Nots*

It was 8:15 when Hector parked the truck in front of Amalia's house. That week was a big week for them. The football championship would be played on Friday, they would have the opportunity to redo their disastrous tests, and it was the day Hector and Amalia would go public with their relationship, in front of *haves* and *have nots*.

They arrived in front of the building of the high school and were hesitant to leave the car, especially Hector. This is because Hector had been around the *have nots* and knew they would face some opposition from them, but nothing compared to his friends, the *haves*.

He knew them and how they could be cruel when they wanted. He looked at Amalia and all he wanted was to protect her, but he knew it wouldn't be easy.

"Do you want to pray?" she asked, feeling his hesitancy.

"Sure," he said, and they prayed together.

School was about to start. She grabbed her backpack, and he had his own backpack and folders. They looked at each other and entered the building holding hands.

The corridors were filled with people despite it being almost time for the classes to start. From both sides, left and right, Hector and Amalia could feel the looks of absolute confusion, shock and unbelief.

He took her to her class before going to his.

"Remember the test after class, ok? Focus on it because we both need this grade. See you later," he said and kissed her discreetly on her left cheek.

"See you later," she answered back.

Both Amalia and Hector had to deal with very unsettling classes. Both of them could listen to people whispering things like, "Can you believe it? It has to be a prank."

Amalia couldn't help but feel a little bit nauseated with the situation and the looks coming from Kat and friends. Even when she looked in Little's direction expecting a kind or compassionate look, she found Little whispering in her direction "What did you expect?!"

The situation for Hector wasn't easy either. JC, Jace and Clay turned their faces away from him, completely ignoring him, which made Hector sad, but not surprised.

He wasn't expecting less than this. Hector was used to facing social pressure since he was in middle school due to his father's position in the town. He knew it would be hard, but he would survive.

When lunchtime came, he went to Amalia's classroom so they could eat lunch together. He arrived at her class and had to deal with Kat and her friends' looks. It hurt him, but at that point, he was more concerned with how Amalia was dealing with it all.

"Maybe we should go to the library instead," Amalia suggested, as she was noticeably uneasy.

"No, Amy. We can do this, ok? It is going to be tough, but it is going to pass. Ok?" he said and convinced her to go to the lunchroom as any other student would.

When they arrived in the cafeteria, it was a little more challenging than Hector expected. When they showed up in the line, people left it as if they had a contagious disease. Amalia felt better when she saw they were serving pasta and meatballs, it should help her to have her favorite dish on such a horrible day.

"No line. More food for us, I guess," he said a little bit tense, trying to break the ice.

"Sure," she agreed, disheartened.

They had their trays and went on to find a place to sit, but suddenly there was no place for them. Jace shook his head. Amalia looked at Little's table and she looked angry. Adam was even avoiding eye contact with them. They were there in the middle of the lunchroom and everyone, absolutely everyone, was looking at them.

They didn't know what to do or where to go when a couple of sophomore students said they were leaving so they could sit at their table. They sat at the table and even Hector felt nauseated by the situation. Amalia looked at her tray, but she couldn't eat.

"Do you think this is all because of Kat?" she asked him with a lump in her throat.

"No, Amy. We caused a huge havoc between *haves* and *have nots*. This is bigger than Kat, believe me." he said tensely.

Hector realized how disheartened she was and held her left hand. As uncomfortable as the situation was, he would rather be there with her in that chaotic situation than without her. Amalia looked him in the eyes and smiled, which was exactly what he needed at that moment.

Little texted Amalia and asked her to sit at her table, but Hector said they shouldn't. Amalia was upset, but Hector asked her to trust him on it. He knew the *haves* pretty well, after being one of them all those years, if he sat at a table with Amalia's friends it would appear as if he chose to be one of them.

Time was passing and Amalia was so sick to her stomach she could not eat a single bite of her food. Suddenly, Alex, Adam, Dan, Alfred and Little showed up at their table. Both of them felt relieved. For Hector having Adam and Dan there and Amalia seeing her friends, it meant a lot to them.

"We came to save you," Alfred said.

"We couldn't let you go through this alone," Alex said.

"Just so you know, I am not happy with this mess, but you are not even eating meatballs, and I know you love them," Little said.

"We are teammates!" Adam stated.

"Go Beavers!" Dan said, being the last one sitting at the table with them.

"Thank you, guys. This is big for us!" Hector said relieved.

"War zone peace!" Amalia said and they all laughed.

They finished lunch and went back to their classes. After the school ended, it was the moment of truth. Hector and Amalia were redoing their tests. Hector went to one room and Amalia to another. Both of them ended up having good second tests and were relieved.

Hector was waiting for Amalia when she left the room. Hector was missing practice that day because of his test. He was going home, but before was taking Amalia home.

Hector and Amalia were leaving the school building when Kat called him in front of the whole school.

"You can stop this prank right now, H. Stop using this girl to get my attention. You have it!" she said, and he could not believe what she had said.

"I gotta go, Kat." he said trying to avoid a confrontation.

"You cannot trade me for her! She is ugly, unclassy, corny and sloppy. How can you be with someone like her?!" she fired off those questions.

"I like her, Kat. Period," he said and left the building with Amalia.

Before Hector dropped Amalia at her house, he made her promise him she wouldn't look at social media. He knew Kat wouldn't accept his answer. She would never take a no for an answer, and she would do everything she could to attack them.

Amalia spent the majority of the night in silence around her family. The day's events left her traumatized. It was hard to receive so much hostility at one time. She went to the backyard and put on a worship song to dance to God. She knew being connected with God would help her to feel better.

Hector arrived home and tried not looking on social media as he asked Amalia not to. Since he missed practice because of the test he went to the basement to exercise. He needed it more than ever. It was championship week, and they needed to win. He had worked too hard to slow down at this point. He went to bed exhausted, said his prayers and asked God to help him to be strong for Amalia. He answered her text before going to sleep.

"Good night, Amy."

Hector & Amalia

Week Three – Day Two - Tuesday

A Cartoon at the Locker

Hector and Amalia went to the library as soon as the school was open. She asked him to go there since she had a surprise for him. They sat in one of the quiet corners and she sent him a login and a password for one social media network. He was hesitant but she guaranteed him he would like it. He did the login and realized Amalia had created a page for them as a couple with all their memories.

He started looking at it and felt touched by it. All their memories were in one place. Their hayride pictures she took while he was embracing her in the back of the wagon. The dinner pictures from the week before, their Thanksgiving pictures and some pictures of when Hector was smiling with one of the kids from the hospital. They have lived so much in so little time, he thought.

"So, did you like it?" she asked in expectancy.

"I loved it, Amy. You are so amazing. I just wish people could see this too. There is not an ordinary thing in you,"

"I also think the same. But you see me, I see you, and God sees us. It is something, isn't it?" she said full of emotions. "I created this page for us, you can also post in there anytime,"

"I will. Thank you. We gotta go now. Time to face reality,"

Hector took a deep breath when he made it to his locker. There was a cartoon on his door. A drawing of Amalia with money signs inside of her eyes saying, "She really loves him." It was implying she was with him because of his money. He felt his blood boil, but Amalia was next to him. She grabbed the page from him, squeezed it and threw it in the garbage.

"Who did this?!" Hector asked, raising his voice.

"It is not worth it!" she said, trying to calm him down, but even his breathing was altered.

She went to her locker and found other papers in there. They were together and before Hector could see them, she squeezed the pages without even looking at them and threw them in the same garbage can she had thrown his.

On the way to her classroom they ended up arguing about it.

"You are so passive! These papers should be at the principal's office, not in the garbage can!" he said, upset.

"You are giving them exactly what they want. They want to provoke you, to mess up with your feelings and look how you are now! If they realize this messes up with you, they will never stop doing it. Ignore it and it will go away," she stressed.

"You're too passive. I can't stand that!"

"Trust me. Years of bullying. I know what I am talking about," she said, and they realized they had arrived at her classroom.

"See you at lunchtime. Do not throw my paper in the garbage again, ok? It was *my* paper, I wanted to decide what to do with it!" he said upset and left.

Amalia entered the classroom, and she was so upset about the argument she had with Hector she didn't even notice if anyone in the class was giving her a bad look. At that point, she just didn't care.

She texted Hector, apologizing. He was right. She knew she wanted to prevent him from reacting badly, but he was right, it was his note, good or bad. She didn't have the right to throw it in the garbage.

"Sorry. Won't do this again," she wrote to him.

"Thank you. You are probably right. It is a trap. Be there for lunchtime," he finally answered.

Despite the early intense beginning of the day, lunchtime was smoother than the previous day. The peace table of the cafeteria was settled. The division and war between *haves* and *haves not* had a break in there. Dan, Adam, Little, Amalia, Alex,

Alfred and Hector spent lunchtime talking about movies, music and of course, sports.

Amalia

Week Three – Day two – Tuesday

Dents in the Bike

Ben de Souza showed up after school to pick Amalia. He insisted on picking her up since they were going to pick up her bicycle at Tim's shop. She got in the car, and they went to the shop. As soon as they arrived there, Tim took them to a private area where the bike was.

"So Tim, can you explain to my daughter what happened to her bike?" Ben asked and Tim looked at Amalia and Ben, back and forth, trying to decide what to say or how to say.

"You know I worked in forensics before retiring, right? After retiring, I opened the shop, you know all this. I hope you don't be upset with me, but I had to tell your dad," he said, and Amalia froze.

"With the experience I have, I know the dents in this bike were not caused by a fall or accident. It was caused by a car. A car hit you, and well, I am leaving you to talk to your dad," he said and left, leaving Ben and Amalia alone.

"Was it Hector, wasn't it? You didn't tell me because you wanted to protect him. Why did he do this to you? Was he drunk? Or on drugs?" her father accused.

"No, no and no to all your questions! He has nothing to do with it! He wanted to take me to the hospital and to the PD, I was the one who didn't want to! I am sorry I lied, but he had nothing to do with it," she explained passionately what happened.

"So, who did it?" he asked assertively.

"Kat," Amalia admitted.

"James' daughter?! Why in the world did she do this to you?!" he asked in absolute shock.

"Because I caught her cheating on a test, and I was silly enough to imply I knew it. She hit me with her car and broke my phone," she said finally as the words were not coming out of her mouth, but from her chest.

"Oh my goodness, she tried to kill you! I knew this would happen. These *have* kids are raised without any sort of limits. One day something like this would happen! Are they raising psychopaths or kids?!!" Ben busted still in shock. "And where does Hector fit in this story?"

"I never asked the details, but I guess he was passing by and saw it happen. He was the one who helped me. He was really upset and wanted to testify in my favor. I was the one who didn't want to mess with it."

"I hope he is still up for it because we are going to the police right now. I am getting a lawyer, and we will press charges against her," he was furious.

"I am not doing it! I don't want to do it! How hard is it to understand I don't want to go through this? Kat will have her reward one day. I am not doing it. There's only six months of high school left. I am not messing up with it!"

"I don't know if I have a good feeling about this relationship anymore. These kids are dangerous and off limits," Ben said, concerned about her relationship with Hector.

"You can't shield me forever, dad." she pointed out and he went silent.

Hector & Amalia

Week Three – Day Two - Tuesday

A Painful Bingo Night

Hector has just left the shower. He was getting ready to go to church bingo with Amalia. He bent to pick up his sneakers and he could feel the pain in his body. While he was practicing that afternoon, he had to deal with things he never imagined. Jace and Clay, whispering the words "Traitor" every time they came close. They took every opportunity in the practice to hurt him. There were plenty of elbows, kicks and punches when they piled up, while Hector was just trying to survive the practice.

He touched the parts of his body which were sore and hurting. They probably would turn into bruises the next day.

"This is the last week, H. Last week. Hang in there. It is almost over," he said to himself while he looked at himself in the mirror.

He arrived to pick Amalia up and on the way to bingo she told him her father found out about Kat. As expected, she said Ben didn't like the story, but he ended up accepting her choice of not pursuing it legally.

They arrived at the church and five minutes later, Ben and Emilia arrived too. Amalia was surprised to see her parents at the bingo, but Hector could feel Ben's look observing him.

"Great! We are back to square one," Hector's thoughts exactly.

Hector tried to show he was fine during bingo, but every time he moved a bit it hurt. It hurt and he couldn't complain. He kept thinking it would be over in a week, while Amalia was back to her bingo winning streak and won twice that night. She was so happy about it she didn't realize he wasn't doing very well.

"Too hot for long sleeves, don't you think?" Ben asked him after bingo ended.

"It was not a good choice, sir. That's for sure." Hector agreed, even though he had reasons for it.

Before he went to bed, he ended up looking at social media. He saw Jace, JC and Clay with the girls, laughing around the firepit in Jace's backyard. The backyard he had been to so many times during his childhood and early teens. They were all there happy, smiling, having a championship week party, and of course he was not invited.

His mind was flooded with so many voices. On one side, he could listen to Amalia's voice. The sweet tone of voice which made him melt every time, her funny faces and her unique humor. On the other side, he could hear Jace telling him there was no need to cause havoc breaking up with Kat. Six more months and they would end high school on a high note, having good memories for the rest of their lives. Only six months, but he couldn't do it. He ended up sleeping thinking about it.

Hector & Amalia

Week three – Day Three - Wednesday

A Rough Morning

Amalia woke up in the morning and she honestly didn't want to go to school. She just felt a knot in her stomach from the fear of what she and Hector would have to face that day. To make matters worse, Little couldn't give her a ride back home since she would be at the robotic championship for two days. She totally forgot about it. She always felt more vulnerable when Little was not around.

And there was Hector. For the first time since they started dating, he didn't message her. They were not okay, and she knew it. All the pressure started to fall over her, and she asked herself how long they would be able to deal with it. She texted him, saying her father could drive her to school. Hector answered a couple minutes later.

"I am already on my way."

Amalia put on an old pair of jeans, a band aid color t-shirt and grabbed her backpack to wait for Hector. Her family surely could tell something was off, but she didn't want to talk about it. It was all quiet until her mother broke the silence.

"I can't do this anymore! What is going on?!" she asked, concerned.

"I am just having a tough week at school. Just this." Amalia said, and her parents looked at each other because they didn't believe her.

"Since you started dating him, I have been worried because of his father. I don't want you dating a man like him and he is his son," her mother voiced her concerns towards the relationship.

Amalia wanted to tell her mother all she was facing had nothing to do with Hector himself, but with how divided the city was. She was going to answer her when she saw Hector arriving in the driveway.

"I gotta go. I will talk to you later," she said on the way out the door.

She jumped in the car. Hector was silent, so was she. He almost didn't recognize her with a bun in her hair, and she looked down and sad. She buckled up and they drove in silence until they arrived at school.

"I hate seeing you sad," he said after they parked.

"I hate everything we are living and dealing with. It is like a nightmare we can't wake up from," she confessed.

"Do you see why I asked you to wait to tell everyone about us? I knew it would be hard, not *this* hard, but I knew it would be tough."

"You were right about it," she had to agree with him.

"Let's keep going, ok? At some point, this has to stop," he told her and touched her face. "Please cheer up, I hate seeing you like this."

"Can you pray for us to survive another day and for God to help us with it? I don't know if I can take it anymore," she asked, and he prayed. They absolutely needed God to help them to deal with it all.

The third day of the week and the same old thing was still happening at school. Notes outside at their lockers, people whispering around them and their only comfort was lunchtime with their friends. Apart from that, they tried to pay attention in class and survive one more day at school.

After school ended, Hector and Amalia received their new test scores for English and Chemistry, respectively. While Hector received the chance of retaking the full test, Amalia received the chance to retake the test for half the points. Hector got an A- and Amalia had C+, which was better than an F for both initially. Hector went to football practice and Amalia went home. She was more positive than when the day started.

Hector arrived home, went to his bedroom and started to study for the classes he had earlier that day. He stopped for a little bit to send Amalia a photo on their exclusive social media page. He posted a picture of her dancing at the cultural fair, saying he was there but didn't want to bother her and her friends.

"You are full of surprises," she answered with a surprise emoji, and he started to laugh.

He was going to answer her when he was interrupted by his father storming the room and coming towards him.

Hector & Amalia

Week three – Day Three - Wednesday

Not His Daughter

Hector had just received a text from Amalia. He was going to answer her when his father stormed the room and was coming towards him in a way he never did before.

"Tell me it's not true, H.! H., please tell me this isn't true! You didn't do this to me!!" Drew said furiously. His breathing was even altered.

"What are you talking about?" Hector asked in panic.

"Is it true you are dating De Souza's daughter?!" Is this true?!" he asked exasperated.

"She is... umm... She is a great girl, dad," Hector said with his heart beating fast.

"I don't care! You could date any girl in this city, any girl, but not his daughter! This man has jeopardized our family for so many years and you date his daughter?!" he said and sat in Hector's bed with his breathing totally out of control.

"You are going to break it off with this girl tonight. You hear me? You are going to break up with her tonight."

Hector could not believe what was going on. He just couldn't. He felt as if he was hit by a car and hadn't even realized it.

Some many times he roleplayed this in his mind. The moment he would say to his dad he was dating Amalia, but he never saw things coming the way they were.

He never saw his father that way. Never. He didn't want to make things worse but definitely, didn't want to break up with Amalia.

"Sorry dad, but I am not doing it. I am not," Hector said with a lump in his throat. He never had defied his father as he was doing at that moment.

"How can you do this to me?!" he asked in absolute shock.

"Because you always taught me to fight for what I want, and I want to be with her!" Hector answered back and his father started to look sick. Hector's mother, who was listening to the argument, entered his bedroom.

"Please leave this room now, H. Call Dr. Jeff now, please. Ask him to come here. And do not dare leave this house. I may need you," Elinor, his mother, instructed.

Hector left the room feeling guilty and concerned about his father. He could not believe the argument he just had with his father. It was intense. It was raw and now he was full of concern and guilt. He called the doctor, but it went to voicemail.

The phone rang and it was Amalia. She said something about her father, but all he could think about was his own.

"Amy, I can't!" he said and hung up on her.

He finally talked to the doctor, and he was on his way. He was in his brother's room and was in panic that something could happen to his father due to their argument. He told his mother the doctor was on his way.

"Don't leave the house. I may need you," she answered, and he was happy his brother was at church, not at home that night.

Hector just hoped the doctor would arrive on time. He heard a noise in the driveway curb, a noise of a car parking at their house. He thought it was the doctor, but it wasn't.

"Drew! This has to stop right now! Tell *your people* to stop messing with my daughter!" A male's voice screamed outside the house.

Hector knew that voice very well. Now he knew why Amalia tried to call him. She was trying to warn him her father was on the way. Hector hurried up and went downstairs. Ben continued to yell and call Drew to talk to him. Hector opened the door and asked him to stop, as it wasn't a good time, but he continued calling Mr. Larkin.

"Hiding behind your son, Drew?! I won't accept what *your people* are doing to my daughter, and I won't leave here until I talk to you!" De Souza insisted.

Andrew Larkin was so angry that Ben de Souza had the audacity to make a scene at his front door, he started to feel good again. The adrenaline which came from hearing De Souza yelling at his house pumped his energy levels and improved his wellbeing. He was definitely ready for that talk.

"Stop yelling at my door, Ben!" Drew said, opening Hector's window to answer him. "H., open the door and take him to my office. It is *time* we have this talk!"

Ben and Andrew

Week Three - Day Three - Wednesday

The Talk

Andrew Larkin entered his office, and he found Ben de Souza standing there, waiting for him. He went behind his desk and sat. He had told Hector to cancel the doctor's visit because he was feeling well and asked him to bring some water and close the door.

Hector brought them water and his father told him to leave them alone. Drew actually had to tell him twice so he would leave. Elinor also opened the office door in disbelief. In a minute, he couldn't breathe and there he was talking with the man whom he had the most disagreements with in his lifetime. Drew asked his wife to close the door and leave the room since he didn't want to be interrupted.

"Sit," Drew said, and Ben didn't. "Please," he asked him politely and Ben did this time.

Drew drank some water, offered some to De Souza, who didn't accept the offer. Both of them were getting ready for the conversation they couldn't avoid anymore. Larkin took a deep breath.

"What was this nonsense you were talking about, that *my people* were bothering *your* daughter?"

Ben started saying that it came to his attention there have been offensive posts towards his daughter. The pastor from his church showed him the posts because he was worried about Amalia's emotional wellbeing. Ben also told Drew he was sure Kat was the one behind it.

"If it were your daughter, you wouldn't like it either," Ben stressed.

Ben put some of the posts he printed at the church on the top of Drew's desk so he could see it.

"To begin with, I am not happy with this relationship, not at all. It is not going to work for many reasons, but I understand you as a father are angry. These posts are unacceptable. We can't accept it, period," he said in shock with the pictures on his desk.

Andrew kept looking at them. It couldn't be from one of the *haves'* kids.

"What makes you think it is one of us who is doing this? Why couldn't they be from one of yours? Maybe someone is envious of your daughter dating a rich and popular guy," he threw out this possibility.

"If Kat was able to hit my daughter while she was riding her bicycle and break her phone so Amalia wouldn't tell about her cheating at school, why wouldn't she be able to do that?" Ben asked and Drew was absolutely offended.

"I've known Kat since she was a baby, that sweet girl would never do such a thing!"

"Why don't you ask your son who saw the whole thing? You didn't know this either, did you?" Ben said and chuckled.

"You know nothing about these kids, do you Drew? Jace and JC were already seen with a drug dealer. They are always vandalizing the city, and I am sure they beat your son up in practice to punish him for dating a *have not*," Ben revealed to him what he suspected was going on with Hector.

"This can't be true! How do you know this?" Drew asked in disbelief.

"H. was at church last night with a turtleneck, Drew. A turtleneck! And he was grunting every time he moved. You don't need to be too smart to put two-and-two together," Ben pointed out.

Drew called Hector to his office. Hector entered the room, and his father asked him to close the door. In the beginning Drew thought Ben's theory was absurd, but on the night before he asked himself the same question. Why would Hector be wearing a turtleneck when it was a warm night? Now Hector was wearing a black long-sleeved shirt and a sweatshirt on the top of it.

"Pull your shirt up, H." Drew told his son.

"There is no need for it, sir. I don't want to," Hector said, embarrassed.

"If there is any respect left in you for me, you are going to pull this shirt up," Drew said, leaving him no choice but to do it.

Hector raised his shirt and Drew grasped in shock. There were bruises all over him. From the top of his ribs to his stomach, and all over it.

"It was just regular play, just this," Hector said, trying not to make a big deal out of it.

"Oh c'mon, H. How old do you think we are? Five?! Ben and I've been there. This is not regular. They did it on purpose and you know it," Drew said in shock and turned to Ben.

"You are right. It has gone too far. It needs to stop before something worse happens."

"You don't have to do anything. There are only two more days, and the championship will be over," Hector said, trying to avoid more problems.

"This is a big dog fight, H. You stay out of it, ok? Ben and I will work together. And now you have my blessing to date his daughter. I want to see who is going to mess with both of you now," Drew said, and he saw a smile on Hector's face.

Andrew Larkin accompanied Ben de Souza to the front door.

"Thank you," De Souza said sincerely.

"I am the one who needs to thank you. They could have hurt H. more,"

"I did this for Amalia but also for H. too. He is a good kid, Drew."

"I have heard good things about her too. Have a good night, Ben. I still need to make some calls." Drew said and went back to his house, while Ben entered his truck to go back home.

Hector & Amalia

Week three - Day Four - Thursday

Light in the Tunnel

Amalia woke up with a good feeling since she had talked to Hector the night before. She was relieved to know her father and Drew Larkin not only survived a conversation alone, but also were working together in order to reduce the division which had happened in the town.

It was also a relief to know Hector's father not only approved of their relationship, but also invited her to have dinner at their home that evening.

Hector arrived at her house to take her to school, and they couldn't hide how happy they were. Finally, there was a light at the end of the tunnel. There was hope. Hope for them, for Trendville, and for Cotton County.

"That's the Amalia I fell in love with," Hector observed, seeing her smiling.

"God has heard our prayers." she said feeling emotional.

"I guess He did," he said, leaving Amalia's house curb.

Drew was a man of action. Nobody was expecting it, but he showed up at the football practice with a lawyer and a cameraman to film the whole practice.

Drew Larking talked to Jace and JC. Told them it was always good to film games and practices because if there was a need for legal action in the future everything would be documented. This was enough for them to not lay a finger on Hector.

He also talked to Kat and told her he knew everything. He knew her father would be very disappointed in her if he found out all the things she had done to reach her goals.

"You should be embarrassed to support Hector dating that classless girl instead of me. We had plans for the future. Good plans for our families and businesses. Now it is all gone. And you are supporting this madness," The true Kat came out.

"You betrayed us, and I won't stop until my father breaks his partnership with you," she threatened him.

The more Kat talked the more Drew knew how wrong he was about her. The sweet Kat he knew was just a façade. James had always been an ambitious man, but had decent values and would never agree with what Kat did to Amalia.

Bottom line, Kat was a kid, and he wouldn't allow her to get under his skin.

"Be careful, Katherine. James has some influence, but he is not above the law. I hope you change your ways. Regards to your father," Drew said and left.

Hector & Amalia

Week Three – Day Four – Thursday

Dinner at the Larkin's

In the evening, Amalia went to Hector's house to have dinner with his family. She was wearing one of the dresses her mom had kept from her youth. She had a scarf around her shoulders and Hector's excitement was visible with her arrival at his house.

"Now I see why my son fell for you," Drew said in a charming way, welcoming her at the door.

"Welcome to our house," Elinor, Hector's mother, welcomed her with her soft and polite voice.

The dinner went well. Elinor was so excited she hired a chef and servers to serve them during the dinner.

The Larkin's residence was so beautiful, spacious and opulent, so different from hers. White marble and gold finishings were everywhere. There was nothing out of place, absolutely nothing. She felt as if she was inside of an interior design magazine.

They sat down and Hector told his mother about Amalia's inclination for art, and that she was preparing for a worship dance competition. She felt she had a chance to win it. Hector also told his mother about her involvement in charity and her passion for design.

"This all seems very interesting," Elinor said and started talking about the projects of charity she was involved in.

Amalia found out his mother and her friends were the ones who made the fall festival happen.

"When we knew Pastor James' church wasn't having one this year for lack of resources we stepped in. I heard people loved it," she said in the same constant soft and polite tone of voice.

Drew and his wife went to sleep and before going to sleep, both were happy with the sparkle and joy on Hector's face. It was good to see him that way.

Amalia arrived home and she went to the backyard despite it being late. She wanted to praise God and worship Him in gratitude for how things were changed in such a short amount of time.

Hector & Amalia

Week three – Day Five – Friday

Championship Night

It was Friday and the moment of truth had finally arrived. It was the Championship's game night. The last chance Hector would ever have to win the championship for Trendville. Amalia arrived with her family to see Hector playing for the first time. She had always wanted to go to a high school football game, but apart from Rafael's games at middle school, she never saw one in person as she was that night.

As always, the Stadium was all divided. *Haves* were all together in their luxury suites, which were not common for high school fields, but it was a reality in Trendville. Their tickets were almost triple the price of the regular ones and there were drinks and snacks in their suites, while the *have nots* were all together in the regular seats.

Amalia received a message from Hector saying she could sit with his family, but she ended up staying with her family and friends. Even at the games people were divided. At least, they were all rooting for the same team. While the game was getting ready to start, Amalia thought of Hector.

"Saying my prayers and reading Scriptures before coach Johnson's talk," his last text she received from him.

While Amalia was waiting for the game to begin, the team was getting ready for the game.

"Okay guys, this is it! This is the moment of truth. We are not here to have fun; we came here to win. Listen to me, I want you to get there and win this title. This is the best team I have had in many years. You have everything it takes to win this game. I know you can do this. So, go there and do it!" Coach Johnson started his speech while they were all standing up together.

"Hector, can you lead us in prayer?" Coach Johnson asked and he promptly accepted.

"Our Heavenly Father, You know everything. You know how hard we've worked to get here. It was a real journey, but You have brought us so far. Now Father, if this is Your will, help us to bring this joy to those who trusted in us, to our families, our friends and our city we love so much. In Jesus name, amen,"

"Amen," They all cheered and started their howling and chanting.

Coach Jonhson called Hector before they left the locker room.

"H, I am not your father, but I want you to know I am proud of you. I really hope you get the Scholarship you want, you deserve it, son! Now, I need you to focus on the game. You are the captain. I already talked to Jace, JC and Clay, whatever move you plan, they will do it. The team lead is in your hands. Be wise, do not let them get under your skin. Bring this trophy home."

The game kicked off and Hector was able to locate Amalia in the crowd because Rafael had a huge poster saying, "Go Beavers" he had made at home. He smiled in their direction in hopes she would see him from the seats, and then, it was time to get serious, and time to focus on the game ahead.

The Beavers had a tough time earlier in the game. They tried to use the same game plan as in the previous game, but it wasn't working. The ball was not getting to Adam. It took time for Hector and the other players to figure out how to attack the other team, but they finally started clicking.

"H., they are covering Adam, so pass the ball to Dan," Jace said despite all their differences, both of them knew they had the same goal, to win that game.

Hector fired the ball and ran across the field to Dan, who shook three defenders and raced to the endzone for a touchdown.

After that touchdown, the Beavers dominated the rest of the game. It was surreal to Hector to watch the clock expire and realize they won the championship. It was hard to believe all he worked so hard for was actually coming true.

They were preparing for the award ceremony to receive the trophy, when two of the most prominent citizens walked on the stage the whole crowd cheered.

The public address announcer announced them.

"Ladies and gentlemen, please welcome Mr. Ben de Sousa and Mr. Andrew Larkin, former captain and offensive lineman, members of the 1999 Beavers Championship Team.

"Wow! This stage brings me so many memories. What about you, Ben?" Drew asked, touched by all the energy going through the stadium.

"Same with me, Drew. But we are here to bring a message to the whole city. A message of unity our city desperately needs. For years Drew and I have let our differences be at the forefront of everything else, and we sadly see the consequences in our city and our youth, which are both divided and can't coexist with differences," Ben said, roleplaying with Mr. Larkin.

"It is time for a change. It's time for hope. It's time to try something new. It's time to be one. We invite all of you, *haves* and *have nots* to become one, as it should be. Congratulations Beavers! We are the 2022 football champions!" Drew announced excitedly.

They left the stage, and the award ceremony started. Hector was the first one to receive the championship trophy as the team captain and Adam received the player of the year award. JC won the best defensive MVP.

After the award presentation, they went and lifted their coach, coach Jonhson, on their shoulders.

After some time, Hector finally had the opportunity to talk to Amalia. Her family congratulated him, Rafael couldn't be more excited, but he finally had the chance to get close to her and quickly kissed her.

"So, what do you think?" he asked her.

"Well, I am dating a champion now, that's a big deal!" she said and smiled in a way that absolutely melted his heart.

"I have a surprise for you later." Amalia said, and he was excited to find out what it was.

Hector went to the restaurant with his teammates and family. Adam and Dan were with them celebrating at the fanciest restaurant in the city called *Palate Pinnacle.* Amalia and her family decided to go straight home and celebrate with him another time.

After dinner was over, he showed up at Amalia's house and she took him to the backyard. He sat at the picnic table, as she asked him to.

"So, this is for my champion boyfriend." Amalia said holding a bag.

She opened the bag, and he started laughing when he saw the juggling pins in it as he couldn't believe she was really going to do it.

Amalia started juggling them and he started laughing nonstop. She eventually changed for the circles and finalized it saying "Ta-da!" for the grand finale and took a bow. Hector clapped and whistled.

"You are amazing, Amy. You are my present from Heaven," Hector said, pulled her closer to him and kissed her.

"You are *my* present from Heaven." she said and kissed him back.

Months Later

Worlds in Transformation

Amalia

A Last Week Before the First Week.

July 30th, 2023.

Amalia was focused on her goal to finish Hector's scrapbook, so he could remember their best moments since their beginning when they started dating. She was sticking to one of the pictures when she saw a car parking in front of her house. It was Little.

"Are you alive?! I haven't seen you for days!" Little said, entering the house and hugging Amalia.

She looked at all the pictures on the dinner table, the stickers and markers.

"How many pages does the Scrapbook have? 300?" she asked impatiently.

"I am on page 12," Amalia updated her.

"12?! For a scrapbook? What are you putting in there that is taking so long? The first bubble gum

H. ate in front of you or a chunk or his hair?" Little asked in a sarcastic way and Amalia ended up laughing.

Amalia laughed because it sounded ridiculous, but also because it was partly true, especially since she added things like the movie tickets they watched, etc.

"I came here today because I have something to tell you. I know we are all going to different universities, but Adam and I, well we are kind of dating," Little said, a little bit embarrassed.

"I knew it! I knew it! I told Hector last week, there was something going on between the two of you!" Amalia said excitedly after the discovery, and Little buried her face in her hands.

"Tell me everything!" Amalia demanded.

"Ha, well, you know me, I am a tough girl, but it has been... good." Little said playing tough, but her eyes were sparkling, and she had a big smile on her face.

Little stayed for a little and tried to help her with the scrapbook, but she quickly grew impatient and ended up leaving after Adam called. She said they wanted to have a double date before Hector and Adam went to their respective universities.

Before she left, Amalia asked Little why she didn't turn in the video she recorded to the principal.

"First of all, I don't believe any type of justice would happen. Kat would probably have a light reprimand and that would be it. Secondly, I pity her. I don't need to cheat and lie to get good grades. I am a real girl with real grades and real friends. She is not," Little confessed, and Amalia smiled, knowing she was at peace with the decision.

As soon as Little left, Amalia went back to her project. She started to separate the pictures by dates, and she was touched by so many of them, like the day she won second place at the worship dancing contest, also the day all the yellow cones survived, and she finally got her driver's license. Her birthday, Hector's birthday and their graduation day at High School were so many beautiful memories, with all being surrounded by their families and friends.

While she looked at the pictures, she realized things would never be the same one week from that point. They would all be spread across different parts of the country, but at least their friends agreed to see each other on the holidays and vacations.

She felt a knot in her stomach as she knew Hector would be in the northern part of the country, far from her. But she said to herself she needed to be happy as she could since her own design major was about to start in two weeks after Hector left.

She continued working in the book until her parents and Rafael arrived from the city.

"Still doing this?! We left and you were doing this. Did you eat something?!" her mother asked, concerned.

"A little, but I will stop and do more later," Amalia said before her mother started talking nonstop.

Amalia returned to the scrapbook after seeing Hector and having dinner with her family. She continued to work on it until she was done. It was around two in the morning when she finished it. She said a quick prayer and went to sleep. Hector was leaving on the next day to go to college, and she wanted to surprise him.

Hector & Amalia

Farewell Time

July 31st, 2023.

After church, they had a luncheon for Hector at Amalia's house. They set a long table in the backyard and Hector's parents and brother were also there. It was beautiful seeing the families interacting and having fun together. Rafael and Hector's brother, Kyle, were playing football on the field, while Amalia and Hector's mothers were in the kitchen talking and setting up the food together.

It was even better seeing Drew and Ben sitting on the backyard chairs and reminiscing about the old days when they played together. While they were having drinks at the table, Hector and Amalia smiled seeing them all getting along.

"Can you believe this is happening?" Amalia asked him.

"Amazing, isn't it?" he agreed.

Before lunch started Hector said he had a surprise for Amalia. He got on his knee and proposed to Amalia.

"Would you marry me in five years?!" he asked nervously.

"Yes!" she said excitedly.

He put a ring on her finger and such an act gave her more confidence they were not only a high school romance but were really focused on getting married one day.

While Hector was playing football with their siblings, Amalia snuck into his car and placed the scrapbook in his truck's back seat, right on the top of one of his suitcases.

The time flew by, and the party was over. Hector said he would rather leave the town from Amalia's house since he had already been to many dinners and had said his goodbyes to the people he needed to.

He hugged Amalia's parents and Rafael, his parents and brother.

"Take care, son. I will be praying for you," Drew said, trying to hold his tears.

His mother hugged him tight, and Amalia was the last one. She followed him to the car, and they kissed.

"I am going to miss you like crazy," she said after kissing.

"I know, but we have a plan, right?" he asked looking into her eyes.

"Let's focus on the plan, ok?" he said, trying not to cry.

He got into the truck, turned on the engine and the truck started to move on.

While he was driving, he could see them getting further and further in the rearview mirror. Hector left, but when he drove through the streets of Trendville, he could not hold his tears.

The running times with his father in the morning, his mother's elegant presence around the house, his brother around him, trying to copy him in everything he did.

The playtimes with Jace, JC and Clay when they were kids. The stadium he had been to so many times. The sound of the crowd during the games. Coach Johnson and his wise instructions.

And of course, there was Amalia. Amalia dancing in the evening, in front of the cottonfield, Amalia talking and looking at him with her expressive looks and her sweet smile.

Amalia with her unique dresses, smelling amazingly after showering with just regular soap. Her wet hair after the shower. Her weird habits and passions. His Amalia.

He wiped his tears and stopped at the gas station to get snacks and drinks before leaving the town. He put the rest of the snacks in the truck and found the Scrapbook Amalia created for him.

He was absolutely touched with their pictures, notes, favorite songs, verses of the Bible and little details only they knew. The last picture was the two of them when they were children with the saying *meant to be.*

He drove a little bit further and stopped right before the city line. It was time. Time to cross the line, time to leave home, time to become the godly man Amalia needed him to be. It was time to grow.

"Come with me Lord and everything will be fine," he prayed and crossed the city line.

THE END

Other Titles from the Author

HOPE (We All Need It)

The Book of the Secrets – Book 1 – Novel

Never an Accident

Faith in the Season

My Prayer Requests Book

2-in-1 Dea A. Myers Book Collection

Hector & Amalia

All titles available at www.deaamyers.com

About the Author

Dea A. Myers is a Christian author who is passionate to positively inspire people. Since starting her publishing ministry, Myers has published three inspirational books, *HOPE (We All Need It)*, *Never an Accident,* and *Encouragement for the End Times.* She has also published her first novel, *The Book of the Secrets- Book I.* The author also has a passion about many forms of art, as witnessed by her holiday e-book, *Faith in the Season.* She has also published a prayer journal, *My Prayer Requests Book* and a book collection called *2-in-1 Book Collection By Dea A. Myers.* In 2024, Myers now releases her second novel, Hector and Amalia, a faith-based teen love story.